THE
NAZ AND ROZ
CHRONICLES

BETHANY-KRIS

Published by Bethany-Kris

www.bethanykris.com

ISBN 13: 978-1-988197-89-0

Cover Art © Sasha Elle

To all the Naz and Roz fans. And Penny, too.

CONTENTS

ONE

Five Years After Naz & Roz …

Roz

Spinning around in her apartment, Roz looked for the box she'd just walked away from not three minutes ago. It was the one with the papers stacked close to the top, and according to the doctor's office that just called … the information she was seeking had been in a file they mailed over the week before.

Unfortunately, her entire place was just *boxes* right now. Boxes to the left, and boxes to the damn right. Problem was, while most of the lower section of boxes had been packed and taped up properly, the ones on top were not. So, it could be in any number of boxes, and Roz just *really* didn't have time to try and go through each box right now because—

The chiming of her phone in the other room had her sighing. That right there was why she didn't have time, probably. She expected it to be one of her handlers for the company calling to make sure she was still on time and didn't need them to send over a driver to bring her to the Hall. Running to catch the phone, she picked it up on the fourth ring just before it would go to her voicemail. Pressing it to her ear, she let out a breathless, "Hello?"

"How interested are you in making a stop in England before heading back to the states, anyway?"

Roz blinked. *"Kyle?"*

Silence answered her back on the other line before the man asked, "How many English people call you with a request to stop in England, Roz?"

It took her entirely too long to blink away the confusion settling in her mind and reply to him. Not that she wasn't happy to hear from her old mentor—she was. Like she would always be whenever Kyle took time out of his *very* busy life to send little old her a message. Roz was getting better and better with this sarcasm thing.

Really, her former mentor didn't call a lot. Usually once a year, but he might call twice if he heard news of something big happening in her career. She knew he kept up with everything—hell, he knew about things happening to her before it was even announced in the upscale music circles. But for the most part, Kyle didn't call a lot and he let Roz have her space. After all, he wasn't her mentor anymore— she had made it to the top of her career like she wanted to be, and he helped her to get her foot through the door.

And now …

Roz turned around to look through the entryway of the kitchen, and peer into the living room where the boxes were stacked up high. A reminder that she had finally decided to choose a different path, now. Something that would take her back home where she wanted to be the very most.

Back to New York.

Back to *him*.

God, she missed Naz all the time.

2

"Did you hang up completely, or what?" Kyle asked.

Roz rolled her eyes and went back to the conversation. "How do you know I'm leaving Australia? You haven't called in eight months, and I only made this announcement two months ago."

"Do I have to call you every time you do something I disagree with, or ...?"

Jesus.

"Kyle—"

"I didn't call to argue about you leaving the Australian company. And even though I don't agree with it," her former mentor quickly added, "I understand your need to do something different. But that's the thing, isn't it? I called a couple of companies in New York when I had a minute last week, and guess what I found out?"

"Probably nothing that I care to hear."

Kyle let out a sigh. "Like I said, I called a couple of companies. The only companies that I know would be worthy of *you* and your talents. Yet, none of the owners of those companies had even heard from you—mind you, they let me know I should pass along the message that if you're looking for something new, closer to home maybe, they are very willing to bring you into the company. You just have to make a phone call to get it done."

That was the thing, though. Five years later, and Roz wasn't sure what she wanted to do. When she played show after show, it started to become the same thing over and over again. The bright lights wore off, a lot like the everything else. Her name had been in lights and was able to shine.

But here she was at twenty-three, and she didn't know if she wanted to keep doing this. What she wanted to do, like she had from the moment she stepped foot on Australian soil, was go home. Constant homesickness wasn't cured by a stage, a shined piano, and a beautiful dress.

She needed Naz more than she got him. He never said a word edgewise to her—never once asked her to come back. Over the last five years, they worked it out. He flew to her, or she flew to him. When he had a job that took him out of country and closer to her, she made sure to head his way if he couldn't come to her. They took vacations to different spots. But typically, they were only able to see each other a handful of times a year, and for the most part, it might only be three or four days at a time.

The last time they had got together for a spread of days was two months earlier during a vacation to Barbados. That was really when Roz cemented her decision to leave the Australian company and head back home. Naz hadn't said one thing about it when she called to tell him after arriving back in Australia. He simply told her to do whatever she needed to do. Her company, on the other hand, tried to convince her to stay a little while longer.

She couldn't ...

It might have affected them—she loved him just as much now as she had when she was a stupid eighteen-year-old girl; she was faithful, and she never questioned if he gave her the same respect because she knew he did. But at the same time, she needed to close some of that distance now.

It'd been too long.

"How about you let me worry about my career?" Roz asked her old mentor. "And you worry about … whatever it is you're doing with your career lately."

"Oh, nasty."

Yeah, well.

Sometimes that was the only way to get your point across to Kyle. He didn't understand anything else. She had to do what she had to do. Simple as that.

"What's in England?" Roz asked, folding her arms over her chest, and heading into the living room. Her gaze skimmed over the tops of open boxes while she still had time, trying to find that fucking *file*. "Because I can promise you it's nothing that will interest me enough to make me stay there, either."

"A prodigy, actually," Kyle said.

Roz stiffened in place. "What?"

"She's sixteen. Typical sixteen-year-old, too. Moody, snappy, and impatient. She doesn't follow direction well, and she's already been expelled from two other prep schools for the musically gifted. Heathrow Prep was her last stop. If she gets kicked out of here— very likely that's going to happen—then she's going to be sent back to New Jersey where her parents have no idea what to do with her. Thing is, it'll be a mighty waste of talent, Roz. She just needs the right person to—"

"Why can't that be *you*?"

"Because I'm a man. She doesn't like … men," Kyle said, his voice dipping a bit. "Seems everyone around this girl is more interested in trying to correct her behavior than trying to figure out *why* she's behaving the way she is. Not that I think for even a second, she would talk to me about it, that's not why I'm calling. I thought …"

"You mean for me to mentor her?"

"Roz, it would be a terrible waste of talent."

"There's more to life than what someone can do with an instrument," she shot back.

Kyle scoffed. "Maybe in your life. Anyway, make the stop in England. Do whatever you gotta do to get your tickets switched around. It'll be what, a couple of extra days on your trip? I'm sure your gangster boyfriend won't mind."

Roz clenched her teeth. "Don't call him that."

"I was kidding."

"Well, *don't*."

Kyle acted like she hadn't said a thing. "Okay, so England is a go, then?"

"Fuck you, Kyle."

He knew she wouldn't refuse. That's why the bastard called. But it didn't even matter. The asshole hung up before Roz could say anything more about the situation. Like a refusal to mentor a girl who sounded like she was troubled and needed someone to help her more than she needed someone to further her musical career.

Roz stared at the dead phone in her hands and glared. *Asshole*. Was that even something she wanted to do, really? Sure, it kind of felt like she had hit an early peak in her career, but was she so *done* with it all that all Kyle thought she was good for now would be mentoring the next young pianist prodigy?

Fuck.

Hormones were a bitch.

Speaking of which …

Roz's eye finally caught sight of the box in question that she had lost earlier, and the file sitting right at the top from the doctor's office. When she'd gotten off stage one night, and promptly puked into a trash can, her handler called in one of the doctor's who worked on call for the company. He came in, drew blood between sets, and sent her back out on the stage to finish her set. The results had been mailed in, but Roz had kind of passed over the file because well, she felt fine mostly. She figured maybe she ate something bad that day, and never gave it another thought.

And then her period was late.

And then she realized no, it'd actually been late for two months.

Since that vacation with Naz.

Picking up the folder, Roz opened it up, and flipped through to the page the doctor's office had told her she would find the information she was looking for. And sure enough, there it was printed in big, bold letters.

PREGNANCY CONFIRMED.

TWO

Naz

"Aren't you supposed to be up in the air right now? Why do I hear—"

"Little change in plans," Roz said.

Naz glanced up from the bathroom sink where he'd been flicking his razor into the basin—fuck, here he was at twenty-five, and his father still bitched when his face wasn't clean shaven. *Made men can't have that, shave it,* Cross would bark. Drove him crazy. "What do you mean, a change in plans?"

"I agreed to make a quick pitstop in England for—"

"Kyle," Naz said dully.

That asshole.

All these years, and Naz still thought Roz's former mentor was a bit of a prick. Not that the guy had ever overstepped his boundaries, or anything, because that wasn't the case. Naz just figured the guy's cocky attitude was little too much to take even when he was in a good mood, never mind when he wasn't. And that was saying a lot considering his father was Cross Donati, and Naz was … well, himself. Cut from the very cloth that made his father, too.

"What did Kyle want that you were willing to entirely change your plans, switch flights, and … when exactly are you going to get into New York, then?"

Because *fuck*, he'd planned to be there to pick up Roz, not some random driver with a car. *He* wanted to be the one to pick his woman up after not seeing her for a little more than two months. Not to mention ... being separated by the world for five goddamn years. This was supposed to be their time—she was finally come back to stay.

He was ready for that, even if he didn't give her an impression that he cared either way. Naz let her know he was happy that she was coming home—because fuck yeah, he was. But he didn't tell her she *had* to come home, and certainly not for him. He refused to step in or step on her dreams in anyway. If she wanted to further her career beyond what she had already accomplished, then he was going to be the first person to tell her to do that.

Even if what he wanted the most was for her to be with him.

"I'm not sure," Roz said. "I switched out the final flight to detour into England. I planned on getting a ticket when I went back to the airport. I really don't plan to stay here very long. A couple hours, maybe. Just long enough to appease Kyle, and then I'm on my way to you, Naz."

He smiled a bit at that.

Still ...

Fucking Kyle.

"What did he want, anyway?" Naz asked.

"Uh ..."

"Roz."

She sighed. "I guess there's a girl he found that needs a good mentor behind her. She's from New Jersey, but she's been placed at the same school I attended until graduation. They don't think she's going to stay there for very long though. Seems she gets kicked out of every school her parents send her to."

Naz straightened against the sink and considered her words for a minute before replying. "Sounds like maybe someone's parents should stop sending their kid to someone else to take care of and start taking care of her themselves. But what the fuck do I know?"

Roz cleared her throat. "I looked into them—called Kyle back the next day to get some information. They're old money from Jersey, and yeah. It could be rich-kid syndrome, but that also just means they have enough money to satisfy a spoiled kid, Naz. Which you know, is exactly what people do when they don't want to deal with a kid they can't handle. They send them away to prep school and give them enough money to keep them quiet until they're old enough to get them out of their hair altogether. Instead, she's been sent to schools for the arts—and they don't bring her home at all. That doesn't explain anything to me. Not why she's rebelling like she's hurting, anyway."

Naz shook his head because yeah, she had a point. And this right here was Roz in a nutshell. He knew now why she stopped in England, and whether she wanted to admit it or not, it probably had very little to do with Kyle. More like, his sweet woman found someone she thought needed help, and just being who she was, couldn't walk away without seeing if *she* could be the one who might be able to help the girl.

How was he supposed to get mad about that?

He couldn't, really.

"All right," Naz finally murmured, staring at himself in the mirror. A few extra hours, that's all. He just had a few more hours than he was expecting to have to wait before he'd have this woman back in his arms—they could start this thing called life together, finally. What were a couple more hours in the grand scheme of things? He could wait that long, surely. "Just call me whenever you're on a flight on the way *here*. So, I know, babe."

"You got it." Roz laughed nervously, adding, "I might have a little surprise for you, by the way."

"Might? Either you do or you don't, Roz." Naz chuckled. "Not that I need anything, babe. Just having you back in New York is going to be enough for me, if that's what you want, too."

"Of course, that's what I want."

"Then that's enough for me."

"Well, we don't really get a choice in this surprise. It's coming one way or the other."

"What—"

"Oh, there's a cab. Okay, I'll call you in a couple hours to let you know the new flight time, okay?"

Naz was still trying to figure out what her *other* words meant. "Roz—"

"Love you, Naz."

He could figure it out later.

"Love you, Roz."

THREE

Naz

"I thought Roz was supposed to be getting in sometime this evening," his father said to his right. "I know it was tonight because you made it very clear that if I called your phone at any point in the next seventy-two hours, you were going to come over here and …" Cross made air quotes as he said, "… personally gut me like a pig."

Not that the threat really fazed his father. Nothing ever did. Naz still tried to give his father a warning every once in a while.

Cross glanced over at Naz with an arched brow. "That is what you told me, wasn't it?"

Why was his father such a prick?

"Rub salt in the wound, Dad," Naz muttered. "I told Ma why Roz was going to be late, so don't act like she didn't tell your nosy ass the first second she could."

"First of all—"

"You are nosy," Naz interjected.

Cross scowled. "And secondly—"

"You gossip like a fourteen-year-old girl at her first dance," Naz said.

"I don't know where you get that mouth from. It doesn't come from me."

Naz laughed. "Lies."

"All lies," the man in the wicker chair to Naz's left said with a smirk around the cigar in his mouth. Zeke side-eyed Cross like he was waiting for his friend to punch him for that comment. "You should have seen your father when you were all of maybe … five, Naz, and you told the neighbor to fuck right off, then when he wouldn't throw your ball back across the street for you. Your mother was horrified—your father?"

Cross grinned. "I remember that."

Zeke shook his head. "Cross laughed and told the asshole the same thing you did before he took you to the mall and bought you a whole bag of balls to throw in the guy's yard. We sat on the porch and watched while you threw your balls across the street, and he called the cops on a five-year-old. So, there's that."

"Good times," Cross said to himself.

"He knows exactly where you get it from."

Naz found it slightly amusing how the two of them could converse with him, each other, and also pretend like they were having a conversation with themselves all at the same time. He was used to this kind of shit from his father, and Cross's best friend, though.

That was funny, too.

He'd been with Roz for five years, and he still didn't see Zeke as her father first. He still just saw his Godfather as his father's best friend, and her father second. He supposed that was because Zeke never stepped in on Naz's relationship with Roz. He just stepped back and let the two of them figure out whatever in the hell they needed to figure out.

He appreciated it, really.

Cross looked over at Naz. "Do you know when she's getting in, then?"

Naz sighed and shook his head. Resting back in the wicker chair, he stared up at the blue sky and wished he was on his way to the fucking airport right now to pick Roz up. After all these years apart … this was supposed to be their time.

"No," Naz said, trying hard not to grumble.

And failed like a fucker, too.

"From what I know," Zeke started to say.

"Nobody asked you."

Cross reached over and smacked Naz hard right in the middle of his chest. "Watch your fucking mouth, there."

Naz rubbed the aching spot and scowled. "What were you going to say Zeke?"

Roz's father chuckled. "I was saying … that from what I know, she won't be too long in England, right? Just a pitstop. She'll be back in New York before you even know what's going on. You are not the only one here who wants to have her back in the states, Naz."

Felt like it sometimes.

He didn't say that out loud.

The thing was, Naz didn't mind letting the two of them think he was just sour over the fact that he was going to have to wait a bit longer before Roz was back in the states. That wasn't his biggest issue with this whole thing at all. He was more concerned with his last conversation with her, and how she kind of left him wondering about something she'd said rather flippantly.

Yet, it stuck in his head.

Well, we don't really get a choice in this surprise. It's coming one way or the other.

He didn't know what in the hell that meant, and it wouldn't leave him alone. It had stayed in the back of his mind ever since he hung up the phone with her. If she had something to tell him—a surprise, right, so that must mean it was good—then he wanted to know it.

Naz wasn't fucking known for his patience.

To say the least.

Something else he got from his dad.

"I have a question," Naz said.

"Hmm?" Cross glanced over at him over the top of the beer bottle he'd tipped up for a drink. "What's that, now?"

"What kind of surprise just comes, and you don't really get a say in it one way or another?"

He didn't expect his father to know what in the hell he was talking about. He figured Cross would just give him one of those looks. Like his dad was silently telling him to stop acting like a fucking idiot. It wasn't like he gave any context to the question to explain it, but nonetheless, he wondered if he might get an answer that would ... well, give him something more to go on about Roz's statement.

"Like a happy surprise?" Cross asked.

Naz shrugged. "Yeah, sure, why not."

"Uh," Cross said, his brow raising. "I can only think of one thing, really."

Zeke laughed and blew out a heavy cloud of cigar smoke. "Me, too."

The two friends passed a look between one another.

"You thinking the same?" Cross asked Zeke.

"I mean, I got two, just like you."

Cross nodded. "Yeah, we're thinking the same, then."

Naz's brow knotted in his confusion. "Then why can't I figure out what that kind of a surprise it would be?"

"Because you've never experienced it, Naz."

His father's words sounded so simple.

He didn't think it was.

"So, what is it?" Naz asked.

"A baby," Cross murmured. "That's the only kind of surprise that ever came for me when I wasn't expecting it and didn't get a choice one way or the other."

"Me, too," Zeke echoed.

Naz froze.

His gaze zoned in on the wall of trees at the other side of the back of his parents' property, and silence surrounded him. Actually, he could hear Zeke and Cross talking ... but he wasn't really listening.

Was that what it was?

Was Roz ...

Pregnant?

He knew it was possible, but unlikely. And he was only saying that because he knew she kept up on her shots, and the last time they had been together was two months ago on their vacation. But at the same time, he knew that didn't make a difference. It took once for a birth control to fail. It took one time to get pregnant.

That's what happened when people had sex.

Babies.

He was a fucking genius.

He knew how bodies worked and what happened when people had sex. He was very well aware that for any number of reasons, no matter how perfectly birth control had worked previous times, that it could fail. He also knew that there were a number of reasons someone might not have realized they were pregnant right away. He knew all of these things, but he didn't want to think about them unless he was looking at Roz, and she was confirming it.

Pregnant …

It was always a possibility.

"Naz?" he heard his father ask. "You all right?"

He couldn't get out of that chair fast enough, saying, "I gotta go."

"Wait, what the hell—"

"I gotta go," he repeated, already heading across the back yard and leaving his father and Zeke behind him. "Later."

"Naz, what is wrong with you?"

"I gotta go!"

Was that what it was?

Was she pregnant?

Naz needed to know now.

FOUR

Roz

"Took you long enough."

Roz openly glared at the man standing behind the door of his flat. She didn't even try to hide the fact that she was annoyed and holding two pieces of luggage. "No, Kyle, the appropriate way to greet someone at your door is with a hello, and then you take my fucking luggage off my hands. Try that."

Okay, wow, hormones.

Roz was not the type to be snappish, but apparently today was not the day to test that theory out. To be fair, she had just spent far too many hours in the sky, in a tin box, flying through clouds with an angry baby—poor kid—a few rows back, and a man beside her who wouldn't quit talking even when she basically put her headphones in and turned her music up loud enough that the flight attendant asked her to turn it down.

Add onto that the fact that she had barely made it through the entire flight without puking her guts out because now that she knew she was pregnant, her morning sickness seemed ready to make itself known again. Which didn't make any sense because most of her flight had not even been in the morning.

But that was pregnancy, apparently. Nothing was like you thought it would be. Well, according to the book she downloaded on her e-reader to read during the long flight. All it really did was scare the shit out of her for several reasons. Fun, huh?

It hadn't been a good flight.

To say the least.

Kyle leaned against the doorway and arched a brow. "What bee crawled up your ass?"

Roz sighed. "Just … take my bags, will you?"

He did as she said but gave her a look all the while. He kept that up until he'd dragged her shit inside the flat, and had it resting against a wall.

"Why did you lug those with you, anyway?" he asked.

Roz shrugged. "Because I don't intend to stay here, Kyle. I wasn't getting a hotel for the night when I knew that it would be pointless. I want to be on another flight before the sun sets here. Got it?"

"Listen, this prodigy—"

"Sounds like a troubled girl who needs a therapist and a good support system, not someone to put her in front of the piano and make her play, Kyle."

He scowled. "Listen, we're not the same."

"I have no idea—"

"Artists, Roz," Kyle said, clearly over her attitude. "we're not the same. Sometimes, what we need is an outlet. And our outlets are not like other people's outlets. We don't beat out our problems in a gym or drown it in food while he binges a television show. We have something better—the chance to use that pain or whatever it is and create something amazing."

"I've never used my music for that."

Kyle rolled his eyes as he turned his back to her and headed for the kitchen area of the loft. "Of course, you didn't. I didn't say all artists are the same, Roz. Just because you haven't experienced something traumatic in your life to focus your music on doesn't mean the rest of us are going to be the same."

She stilled and considered his words.

"Is that what you think it is?"

"What?"

Roz followed Kyle into the kitchen and watched him as he pulled a glass goblet from the cupboard. Then, he went in search of something else. Alcohol, it seemed, if the crystal bottle he pulled from a top shelf in his cupboard was to be believed.

He poured himself a glass and downed it in one go. Roz raised her brow in silence, half amused, and half concerned. With Kyle, sometimes, it could go either way. For as long as she had known him, he had ... well, most people would just call them demons, maybe. Something that never left his mind and left him troubled day in and day out. He dealt with it the best he could, but that didn't change the fact something had happened to this man.

Kyle waved at the bottle of bourbon. "You want a drink?"

"First, not on my worst days would I drink bourbon," she returned, "you all act like that tastes good when really, it tastes like death. And secondly, I can't drink, so no."

"Why can't you dr—"

"We're not talking about me here."

Nope.

She wasn't talking about that with him. Kyle was not going to be the first person besides her and the doctor to know she was pregnant. She had a man all the way across the world who deserved to know he was going to be a father before the rest of the world knew it. Roz owed Naz that much.

"So, is that what you think it is with her, then?" Roz asked.

Kyle cleared his throat. "What?"

"Trauma. You think she's been through some trau—"

"I don't make assumptions about others or what they've been through," Kyle said, and then quieter, he added, "but there's a look—all of us who have been through some shit can see it. It's not like everybody else, Roz. We just … know."

Huh.

She wondered … was it true what people said, that lost people found other lost people? Did they just see a reflection of their own experiences and pain in someone else, and know?

She didn't have a clue.

It wasn't the time to ask.

Kyle slapped a hand to the counter and gave her a charming smile. It wasn't lost on her how two seconds ago, the man had looked dark and entirely lost in his head. It was like he put his mask on for her, and just like that, he was fine again.

Or … he looked that way.

In a way, Roz found that concerning. That Kyle was so good at pretending he was okay to everyone else that he didn't even have to try to make people believe it, really. He probably had years to perfect his … mask.

And wasn't that kind of sad?

She thought so.

"Her name is Penny," Kyle said, "and we can go see her anytime."

Roz chewed on her inner cheek. "And then what, Kyle? What happens after I meet her, huh?"

"Guess we're gonna see."

Great.

That didn't sound problematic at all.

FIVE

Naz

"Business or pleasure, sir?"

Naz looked up from the line he'd been standing in for well over an hour to see a customs agent arching a brow at him. Apparently, he was the next to go through—finally, why did customs always have to take forever no matter which country you were traveling into?—the line to get his shit checked.

"Pleasure," Naz replied, smirking just a bit.

Yeah, pleasure seemed like the right way to say it. He certainly had business in this part of the world, but that had nothing to do with why he was here right now. In fact, he might regret this split decision later, but right now, he seriously doubted it.

"Bag on the table—open it up," the agent said with a gloved-wave. "And get your passport out for me, too."

Naz couldn't count the amount of times he had gone through customs in his life. Okay, that was a lie—he absolutely could count it. His genius brain didn't let him forget. He also knew the exact number of countries he had traveled into over the years, too.

It was a lot.

Fun, right?

Not so much.

Naz hefted his small carry-on up to the table and fished his passport out of the back of his pocket and tossed it over for the man to open and look it over. He didn't notice the look the agent was shooting him until he'd unzipped his bag and looked up at the man.

"What?" he asked. "There a problem?"

That was the tricky thing about being who he was, and by that, he meant a criminal. Naz had a rotating folder of identities he used to run guns, but that didn't mean somewhere … in some fucking country, he hadn't gotten caught in some way. Smart authorities wouldn't plaster his picture and real name all over the place. No, they'd just send his information through Interpol, and let it do the work of waiting for him to show up somewhere again.

It was always a risk.

He took it.

The agent raised a brow and set his passport down. "You don't have very many bags if you're visiting the country for pleasure, sir, that's all."

Naz chuckled and nodded. "Well, I don't plan to stay longer than it takes me to find my girlfriend and ask her if she's pregnant."

The agent blinked.

Naz smiled.

His father liked to say the best way to put a person off balance was to hit them with the last thing they expected you to say. Naz figured this had done exactly that for the guy across the table. One step closer to Roz.

Without even looking through his bag other than a quick, cursory check, the man brought out the items needed, stamped Naz's passport, and nodded at him. "You be on your way, then. Good luck;

you're gonna need it one way or another."

Naz laughed. "Thanks."

He pulled his phone out of his pocket as he headed out of the customs area. A quick check of the screen told him what he expected—Roz was still here in England, and she hadn't left yet. She'd been keeping him updated on what she was doing here, and when she expected to leave. She should have left the night before, but apparently, something made her stay.

Naz believed it was the prodigy.

Penny, Roz had texted her name.

That was fine.

Fine and good, really.

Naz was here now, though. Because they had other things to handle—he needed to know if the surprise she was supposed to share with him was the fact that she was pregnant. There was no way in fucking hell he was waiting for her to fly over to his side of the pond to do it.

Nope.

He was here now.

SIX

Roz

"She didn't react well yesterday, what makes you think she'll be better today?"

Kyle passed Roz a look and shrugged. "Hope and blind faith?"

Roz let out a heavy sigh. "You're an idiot."

"And you're not in a good mood again. What is wrong with you?"

Oh, other than the fact she'd barely slept a wink because she knew she should have been in New York by now, and not still in England? Besides the fact that she had a whole freak out moment about the fact she was pregnant because she couldn't even remember holding a baby before? Besides the fact that she hadn't been able to keep down her breakfast this morning?

And that was before Roz got into … Penny.

The prodigy.

The girl.

Something was not right with that young woman, and Roz didn't mean that in a bad way. She meant it in a way that she just thought … she needed help. She was in a bad place and holding onto a ledge by the very tips of her fingers. She didn't know how she knew it, but she did.

That was concerning.

Penny barely spoke, and when she did? God, the girl was angry. Confrontational, mean, and rude. She hadn't even bothered to get out of bed the day before despite knowing they were coming over to visit her. The head of the dorm happened to mention to Kyle and Roz that Penny had almost got into a fight with a girl across the hall, and they were planning a search of her room because they believed she had drugs hidden somewhere in her dorm.

Bad news.

The girl wasn't trouble.

She was in trouble.

Roz didn't know how to explain that to Kyle, though. He figured the girl just needed the right mentor in her life—someone to put her back on the right track and find the reason to make her sit in front of a piano and do the damn thing again.

That wasn't what she needed.

She needed help.

Something was wrong.

It was only once they were inside the dorm and standing in front of Penny's room that Kyle turned to Roz with a frown.

"You know, I can practically feel what you're thinking," Kyle muttered.

"Can you?"

He nodded.

"Then, you won't be surprised when I say this girl needs help that we can't give her," Roz returned. "Ivory, wood, and gloss isn't going to fix the parts of her that have been broken by someone or something else."

"She doesn't have anyone, Roz."

Yeah, she figured that out. Somewhere between the many prep schools the girl had been sent to, and the fact her parents were just willing to keep sending their daughter away instead of bringing her home and getting her help … Roz knew Penny had no one.

"Can we figure out something for her?" Roz asked. "Something to get her … in a place where she can be helped, and do music?"

"Where would you suggest we move her?"

That was the thing … she didn't know.

They weren't Penny's guardians. They couldn't make legal choices for her. They couldn't even bring in a doctor for the young woman without permission to do so. They had very few moves they could make to help her.

It was sad, really.

"Let's just see how she's doing today," Roz said.

Kyle nodded, and knocked on Penny's dorm room door. At the same time, the phone in Roz's pocket started to buzz. She pulled out the phone as Kyle knocked a little harder on the door.

Roz checked the text message from Naz as Kyle continued knocking, and when he didn't get a response from Penny, tried to jiggle the knob.

"It's unlocked. She knew we were coming, I just talked to her an hour ago," he muttered.

Roz nodded, but was still reading Naz's text.

I decided to meet you halfway, babe. I'm at your hotel room. Surprise. See you when you get back. —Naz

He came here?

Jesus.

The man must have been going stir crazy, but just didn't want to tell her.

Roz was about to reply to Naz when Kyle pushed the dorm door open, and peeked his head in, saying, "Penny, are you up, or what?"

"Don't open her door without her permission, that's—"

Kyle's face went white when he opened the door a little more.

"Oh, my God," Kyle mumbled, shoving the door all the way open. Before Roz could even see what was waiting for them behind the door, he shouted at her to, "Call for emergency services!"

She saw what was behind the door, then.

A blue teenager.

Bare arms that she'd kept covered the day before with a long sleeve were now naked, giving Roz full access to see the crisscross patterns of white, pink, and red marks. Old scars, new scars, and fresh marks.

Cuts.

A ripped bedsheet tied to the pipe across the ceiling.

And a toppled over chair.

"Penny! *Penny?*"

SEVEN

Naz

The thing Naz hated the most about countries he wasn't familiar with? The fact that he didn't know where anything was. He swore it felt like the cab he had managed to hail just drove around aimlessly for twenty minutes even though he knew the driver was taking him to the hospital. But to him, because he didn't know any of these streets or where to go for the hospital, it just seemed like the guy was driving in fucking circles.

It was only made worse by the fact that Naz didn't know what in the hell was going on. He'd gotten a text from Roz with the name of a hospital and told him to get there now. He came to England to surprise her, and to get answers … he didn't think his first stop after waiting for her at the hotel would be a fucking hospital.

Was it for her?

Had something happened?

Was someone going to die because they hurt her?

All possible things.

The cab pulled up to the drop off lane at the hospital and put the car into park. Already, Naz's heart felt like it was in his fucking throat. The panic had been ever constant, and all too present. No matter what he tried to get it to leave, it just wouldn't go. He was the calm one in the storm—that's just how it worked for him.

Not right now.

Not when it came to Roz.

He couldn't be anything when he thought something might be wrong with her. That's just not how his brain worked. All the logical shit was there, sure, but it didn't factor into the way he felt at all.

"That'll be—"

Naz threw a handful of bills over the front seat, saying, "There you go."

"Sir, that's too much money."

"Keep it."

Naz didn't even care.

Once he stepped out of the cab, that pressure in his chest got worse. His heart felt like it was about to explode right out of his fucking chest. A car blew its horn at him when he walked in front of it without looking first, but Naz just tossed his hand up as if to say, *yeah, yeah, fuck off.* He had other things on his mind right now.

He couldn't get into the hospital fast enough. He went right into the emergency section because he figured that's where Roz would have come in if something happened ... it wasn't like she had a doctor here to visit, right?

The emergency room was full—not that it was any surprise. It seemed like that didn't matter what country someone was in. The hospital was always at capacity and overflowing. Wait times for fucking days.

Naz was planning on going right up to one of the receptionists, giving Roz's name, and seeing where that got him. All it took was a quick sweep of the people sitting in the waiting chairs for him to find her, instead.

Roz had tucked herself into the corner of the waiting room near a window. She might have seen him coming into the hospital, except she was currently using her propped arm as a pillow to rest her cheek on her palm. Her eyes were closed, and she'd used a windbreaker to cover herself up. Even her knees were tucked in close to her chest.

Naz might have let her rest her eyes, if she was that tired, considering it was only twelve in the afternoon and she was sleeping in bright daylight. But he couldn't because this very moment was the first time he realized she was actually okay. It clearly wasn't her that needed to be brought into the hospital if she was just sitting there sleeping.

"Roz," he murmured, approaching her.

She didn't move until he was kneeling in front of her and had both of his hands on her tucked up knees. He squeezed her legs gently, and her eyes fluttered open. It took Roz a few seconds of blinking to realize she was awake, where she was, and the fact that she was now looking Naz right in the face.

He smiled a bit. "Hey, babe."

Roz wiped a hand over her face. "Hey."

"Pretty sure this wasn't in the plans when you decided to make a stop in England, huh?"

She laughed bleakly. "No."

Naz tipped his head to the side. "What happened?"

She sniffled, and he didn't miss the way her gaze filled with water before she tried to blink it away. Not that it worked. She shook her head when Naz reached up to stroke her cheek with his fingertips, and then brushed a few strands of her hair behind her ear. It wasn't like Roz to get emotional, really. She had her shit under control—it was one of the things he loved the most about her, but when she did let the emotion through … he knew something was up.

Always.

"The girl Kyle wanted me to come meet to possibly mentor?" she asked.

Naz arched a brow. "Yeah, what about her?"

"She's … not well," Roz said, and then she frowned. "And not like physically sick, but … in her mind, Naz. She's got something going on that she's not telling people. I knew it when I met her yesterday, and then today … it just confirmed what I thought."

"I don't understand—"

"She tried to hang herself this morning. We found her in her dorm."

Naz blinked, and his hands tightened on her legs. "I'm sorry."

Roz shrugged. "I think someone needs to tell her that, you know?"

Yeah, he did.

Naz let out a heavy sigh. "Fuck, babe. I thought this was about you, or maybe …"

She eyed him from the side. "Or maybe what?"

"Nothing."

"Naz."

Just the tone of her voice had him chuckling. This woman knew all of his secrets. She could tell when he was trying to hide something, or just avoid it altogether. There was no way for him to ever pull something over on her. His mother liked to say that was the universe's way of kicking Naz in the ass for all the shit he pulled over the years.

And hell, maybe it was.

He loved Roz for it, though.

Instead of telling Roz his suspicions about what he thought her news happened to be, he just looked at her and asked, "Listen, do you have anything you want to tell me right now?"

Roz pressed her lips together. "Maybe, yeah."

"Okay, well maybe that's why I came all the way here. I didn't want to wait."

She laughed but shook her head. "I shouldn't be happy right now. This is not the time to be—"

"You're human, which means you can feel multiple things at the same time. You can feel pain for someone else at the same time you feel joy for yourself for an entirely different reason. That's normal, babe."

She nodded again. "Okay."

"So, any news?"

"Well …"

"Hmm?"

Roz winked. "Seems I'm pregnant."

Naz grinned.

There it was.

He'd been right, and while he had pushed it to the back of his mind to let her tell him so he could feel all that happiness and joy because she told him … now, he was just over the fucking moon.

"Yeah?" he asked.

Roz laughed. "Like eight weeks, I'd say."

"Barbados, then," he murmured.

"Guess so."

His heart was hurting again, but it wasn't for the same reason from earlier. Now, it was because something amazing was happening in his life. This woman was about to give him something incredible.

"I love you," he told her.

"I know—I love you, too."

Naz finally got to do what he'd been wanting to do for two months, then. He pulled Roz into a tight hug and hid her away from the rest of the world. That's how he liked her best, after all. Tucked into his arms, and safe.

She tipped her head back, and that smile of hers clouded his vision. He dropped a kiss to her grinning lips, and then another and another. Until she was smiling against his kiss.

"So, what happens now?" he asked.

"About what?"

"The girl. Kyle. You."

"I don't know, Naz."

Yeah, him either.

EIGHT

Roz

Naz was funny in the way he would much rather rent an Airbnb, even if he was only staying in a place for a couple of days, than a hotel room. Roz never understood why, but that's how it worked for him. She thought it was probably because he didn't feel at home in a hotel room, or maybe because over the years, he'd stayed in a lot of hotels when he traveled. But who was to say?

Nonetheless, when he figured out she wasn't going to be leaving England for at least another week, the first thing he did was call back home, and get things settled there. The second thing he did was get on the laptop, and rent them an Airbnb because as he said, he wasn't sleeping in a fucking hotel.

Roz let him do what he wanted. It was easier, and she really didn't care as long as she had a bed to sleep in. Even better because he was there to sleep in it with her. But Roz also knew Naz wouldn't be able to stay in England more than a week—people were waiting on him back in New York. Responsibilities and duties were waiting on him to get back to what he did best. She didn't fault him for that.

"Okay," Naz said, hanging up the phone he'd been talking into for the last half hour as he came into the kitchen. "All done, babe."

She peered over her shoulder at him. "Great."

"Two weeks from now on Monday, eleven in the morning."

Roz gave him a look.

Naz arched his brow right back. "What?"

"I thought you were going to make the doctor's appointment for a month from now? What if I'm still here, Naz?"

He shrugged. "This was the closest opening that the office in New York had, babe. If you're still here, then we'll figure something out for a doctor here until you get back home again. Okay?"

She smiled.

He really was something else, this man. She was well aware that he wanted her home more than anything. He wanted to put her on a flight today and get her back to New York where they could finally start their life together. She wanted that, too, more than he could possibly know. But there was still a part of her that needed to see things through here first. She needed to make sure that Penny was going to be okay … or she was going to help the young woman to get to that place in her life.

Naz was just … going to let Roz do her thing.

She loved him for that.

Naz slipped around the island and came to stand at her back. One of his arms drifted around her waist, and his hand laid flat to her stomach before he dropped a kiss to the top of her head. She felt her smile grow the longer his kiss lingered. Finally, she tipped her head back, and he dropped a quick kiss to her lips, too.

"How're you feeling today?" he asked.

She shrugged. "Better—I didn't throw up yet."

Yet being the keyword.

It could still happen.

Morning sickness didn't discriminate.

"You need anything, then you tell me, got it?"

Roz winked. "Got it, Naz."

He grinned and dropped another kiss to her lips. Only this time, he wasn't as quick to pull away. This time, that kiss lingered long enough to burn her from the inside out. Just like that, the flames of her lust had been stoked in the right way—enough to make her want to pull this man back to the bedroom and find all sorts of fun ways to spend their morning.

She suspected Naz was feeling the same way given his hands tangled into her loose hair and tugged gently as his tongue struck out against the seam of her lips, demanding she open up for him. God, she loved that, too. Loved the way their kiss always felt when their lips worked against one another, and their tongues tangled to get a taste.

And then a knock echoed through the house.

Naz lifted, pulling away from her kiss with narrowed eyes as he looked toward the hallway that led to the front door. She might have laughed at his annoyance at having been interrupted with her, but she couldn't.

The knocking continued.

Fuck.

Naz gave her a look. "How much do you want to bet that's—"

"Anybody home?"

"Kyle," Naz muttered.

Naz let her go just as footsteps echoed in the hallway of the house they had rented. She gave Naz a look, silently telling him to stay in line. Not that she needed to remind him, but she also knew there was something about Kyle that often put Naz on edge.

She thought it might be because Kyle was the one who constantly reminded Roz that love could come anytime. Her career in music, however, had a time limit on it. There was an expiry date to her talent—something could take away her ability to play, or she may simply just become irrelevant in the world as a pianist.

But love?

Love would always be waiting.

Thing was … Kyle wasn't wrong. She tried not to put love last the best she could—she constantly tried to keep Naz as the center in her life, the one thing that continued to ground her and remind her what was important.

That didn't mean Kyle had been wrong, though.

"There you are," Kyle said as he came into the kitchen, looking only at Roz. "Did you get a visit like I did this morning?"

Roz passed Naz a glance. "No?"

Kyle scowled. "At all?"

"No. What's going on?"

"The Bobbies came around," he said.

Roz's brow dipped. "The what?"

"English police," Naz said from his new spot behind the island. "Better question is why are they making a visit to you, Kyle?"

Kyle stared hard at Naz. "I don't know—you're better acquainted with the police than I am, aren't you? Why don't you tell me why they do the shit they do?"

Roz didn't need to look at Naz to know he was tense, and probably ready to jump across the counter at Kyle. She quickly stepped in to stop that from happening. "Well, you must know why they came around to talk to you—they talked to you, didn't they?"

"It was about Penny."

Okay, that had Roz's attention. She turned around on the stool entirely so that she could face Kyle for this conversation. She had a feeling, just by the way his tone turned thick, that she was going to need to be sitting down and staring at him for whatever he was about to say.

"And?" she asked quietly.

"They wanted to know if she'd ever ... uh, talked to me about her father," he muttered.

Roz took a second before she asked, "Why would they ask about that?"

"She's made allegations while in the ward."

She was cold, now.

Entirely cold.

Too fucking cold.

"What kind of allegations?" Roz asked.

She didn't want to ask.

She didn't want to know.

Still, she felt like she had to.

"That ... uh," Kyle struggled, refusing to meet Roz's stare.

"That kind of allegations?" Roz asked.

"Sexual abuse?" Naz spoke up behind her.

Kyle swore under his breath and scrubbed a hand down his jaw. "Yeah, that's what it sounded like to me. She made some serious allegations when the Bobbies were brought in to talk to her about an investigation, they have for something she did in the dorms against another girl who she had beaten up in the communal showers."

Roz straightened. "Why did she beat up a girl?"

"I don't know. Maybe she said something that triggered her?"

She looked over her shoulder at Naz, but he was staring hard at Kyle. She could tell by the tension in his shoulders, and the hardness of his gaze, that he wasn't pleased. And not because of Kyle, but because of the rest of the information they had right now.

"They don't think she's saying that just because of the investigation about the girl, right?" Roz asked Kyle.

"I don't think so ... but the bigger problem is this isn't their territory," Kyle said, shrugging and looking helpless. "This happened in America—they can't bring charges against an American for something that happened in America. They're referring the case on, but she's underage. They're going to send her home, she'll be in the care of CPS until they get this figured out and—"

"No," Roz said, firmly.

"What?"

"She doesn't need to be in the care of CPS. We can figure something else out for that. She can stay with me and Naz, even. Right?" She looked back at Naz who met her stare but said nothing. When he stayed quiet, she pressed again, asking, "Right?"

"Roz, that girl probably needs a lot of help and—"

"Okay, then we get her what she needs, Naz."

"She might not be comfortable with a man there."

"We don't know that if we don't ask."

"Okay," he murmured, clearly not wanting to fight.

Kyle cleared his throat, bringing their attention back to him. "They kept sending her home, Roz. She'd act out, and they'd send her back. Where he was waiting. I got the impression that the allegations she made indicated it had been a regular thing until she left for school, but it continued through the years. So …"

"Every time she got sent back," Roz whispered.

What kind of father …

What kind of monster?

Roz felt Naz's had find her back, and he said nothing as he stroked her just below the neckline of her shirt. Like she was the one who needed to be comforted then. It wasn't her that needed someone to love them and protect them at all.

She had always had people to do that.

Penny, though?

Clearly never had anyone.

NINE

Roz

The sixteen-year-old tucked into the window bench, overlooking the backyard of the infirmary where she had been placed—a temporary hold until, one, she was no longer a threat to herself, and two, they figured out what to do with her by placing her somewhere safe—didn't even acknowledge Roz when she approached. She didn't take it personally. It was quite obvious that Penny Masterson had plenty of things on her plate to deal with it, and Roz bet she was simply a very small portion of that.

"I noticed they have a music room down the hall," Roz said.

Penny didn't look away from the window.

Roz didn't let the silence bother her too much. Stuffing her hands into the pocket of her dress, she peered around the quiet room that seemed to be some type of area for communal gathering for the patients. Stark white, the walls and floors gleamed. The light fixtures above were the same bright white and flush with the ceiling. A setting of couches and chairs had been set up in one corner next to a row of bookshelves, and another sitting section in the other corner faced a large flat-screen television. Toward the west side of the room, hallways leading further into the complex showcased a few scattered people moving from what seemed to be different rooms.

A single woman wearing gray scrubs came out of the hallway but didn't even pass Roz a look before she disappeared behind a door where a wall of Plexiglas windows gave them a clear view of the many medications sitting on shelves.

That was the only indication this place was something different than it appeared on the surface. Specifically, the institution handled teenagers from thirteen to eighteen—on their eighteenth birthday, if still here, they were transferred to a different institution with adults—dealing with mental illness.

Those illnesses ranged from behavior, eating, and other disorders, not limiting it to just that, they also handled cases like Penny.

"Why are you here?"

Roz jumped a bit at the question, surprised the teenager had even spoken to her at all. She came to visit three times in the last week, and each time, Penny said nothing. Each time, she sat in this same place, stared out the window, and stayed silent.

She wasn't willing to give up, though.

"And where is your shadow?" Penny asked when Roz didn't answer her right away.

"My shadow?"

"Tall guy," Penny said, "dark hair, never leaves your side when you're here, and glared at a guy when he checked you out."

Roz blinked.

Had Naz done that?

Because only Naz had come with Roz to visit Penny, although he stayed back as to not intrude on their conversation ... or rather, the total fucking lack of it, for the most part.

"Naz ... he's my boyfriend," Roz said. "And he thought maybe it would help if he didn't shadow me, as you might say. Because maybe he was making you uncomfortable."

Penny made a face and looked back to the window. It struck Roz, then, how childlike Penny seemed in a lot of ways. She was small featured, and small-bodied. With her hand propped up to use it as a rest for her chin while she stared out the window, she almost seemed like a little girl. Put her in a white dress, and wipe the red lipstick stain from her lips, and she could probably pass for a twelve-year-old.

It was disconcerting.

"He doesn't bother me," Penny said, "I can tell when they're … bad. I see it in them. There's a way they look at you. They're all the same, you know."

"I don't, actually."

She couldn't imagine the horrors this girl had gone through. She couldn't begin to consider what it was like to look at every strange face that passed you by, and think, *is he like one of them; is he a monster, too?*

"I haven't used the music room," Penny said.

So, she had been listening to Roz. That made her wonder, what else did the girl listen to when people thought she wasn't paying attention?

"Why not? Their baby grand is beautiful."

"Needs a good tuning," Penny replied dryly.

Roz laughed. "I am sure Kyle could come in and—"

"He's not like them, but he's the same as them in that he wants something from me. It might not be the same thing—he's not like *that*," Penny said, looking back at Roz with her wide, blue eyes that just always seemed so fucking haunted. "He's not like that, but he wants something from me, he's only interested in what he can get from me."

She blinked.

"And what is that?"

"For me to play," Penny said simply. "The piano, I mean. That's all he's focused on. It isn't the same thing as the rest of them, but it's still something."

"I promise Kyle isn't only interested in making you play. That was a big factor that drew him to you, and he would still love to see you play at a piano, but it's not at all the only thing he cares about, Penny."

"Mmm."

The noncommittal sound made Roz sigh quietly.

"But you," Penny said, looking Roz over with a pensive stare, "I don't know about you. I can't figure you out. Everybody always wants something from me—they don't care how they get it, but I can't find what it is you want. And I don't like that."

"Nothing," Roz whispered.

Penny raised a brow in silent question.

Roz shrugged. "I just want to help, Penny."

That was the reason she was still in this fucking country. Instead of being at home, telling her parents they were going to be grandparents again, or letting Naz share the news with his parents. It was why she had allowed Naz to buy tickets that he had to cancel last minute because she couldn't zipper up her luggage knowing this young woman was stuck in this place, hurting and broken.

"I'm angry," Penny said.

Roz nodded. "I don't doubt that."

"No, you don't get it. I'm mad, Roz. At everything—at the world. All the time, it never leaves. It's right under my skin every waking moment of my life. I tried to cut it out, and I can't get it to leave. I look at people like you—happy and good. There's not things in your head that aren't right. There aren't people in your life who hurt you when they were supposed to love you. And I'm so fucking bitter about it. I look at you, and all I see is everything I can't ever be. And that makes me angry. I don't want to be angry anymore. I don't want to be anything anymore."

"Penny—"

"And you think you can help?"

"I think you need someone who is willing to try," Roz replied. "So here I am, willing to try. I'm not asking for your permission to do it because if it was left up to you, I don't think you would let anyone help. And yeah, I'm here whether you want me to be or not."

That quieted the girl.

Finally, Penny muttered, "They're saying I have to go back to the States … for a lot of reasons."

Yeah, Roz knew that, too.

Because Penny needed to bring charges in the country where the assaults happened. Because she wasn't a citizen of this country, she couldn't be placed with a family or conservatorship here. And there were more details that just ... muddied all of this up.

"I applied to foster you when they bring you back to the states," Roz said quietly.

Penny's head snapped up. "What?"

"It was me, or a random family. A random foster home. I am here to help," Roz said again, "whether you want me to or not."

"Oh, I bet Kyle will love that," Penny sneered under her breath. "Put the prodigy in with the washed-up prodigy, and he gets exactly what he wants."

Roz brushed the girl's attitude off.

Mostly.

"I have spent the last several years headlining one of the biggest orchestra companies in the world, and I chose to leave the company because I want to begin my life with a man who waited for me despite all the odds," Roz said, "and I truly don't give a single shit if you never put your fingers back on the ivory again, Penny, but in case you haven't figured it out yet, lashing out to hurt me doesn't actually fix you."

Penny wouldn't look at her, but her shoulders sunk a bit. "Sorry."

Roz decided to go in a different direction with the girl. "How are you feeling about the fact they're going to make a second formal statement about your father's abuse to US officials once you're back home? I imagine you don't want to go through that a second time."

Something akin to a bitter sneer curved the girl's lips.

"What is that for?" Roz asked.

"You think it was just my dad?" Penny gave Roz a look over her shoulder, and in that moment, it felt like her heart fell to the floor and shattered. "It's more than just him. There are a group of them, Roz. It's a network. And I am not the only one they did it to. We're a commodity to them ... something to be traded, kept, or borrowed. He only sent me away because I was getting too old, my body changed, and I was getting louder. I was causing problems—I was a problem. That's why they started sending me away."

She felt sick.

"I haven't broken the surface yet," Penny continued, "but when I do, nothing is ever going to be the same, and that is what scares me."

"A network," Roz echoed.

Because she was still stuck on that.

Why would this girl lie?

"They're everywhere. But you're not like me, so you can't see them. Monsters are very good at hiding in plain sight."

TEN

Naz

"And this is the room where Penny will be staying, correct?" the woman CPS had sent in to do a walk-through of Naz's Manhattan penthouse. Now, Roz's penthouse, too.

"That's right," Roz said. "She's sixteen—she needs privacy, and her own space to be alone in when she feels the need, doesn't she?"

"Being that she's a suicide risk—"

"She is still sixteen."

The woman nodded and scratched something on the paper in her hands before looking back up at Roz. Then, her gaze drifted to where Naz was lingering at the end of the hallway, closer to the sitting room in the penthouse. The wall of glass windows behind him sat in front of a baby grand that had once been his grandfather's.

Naz tried not to feel edgy when the woman looked him over, but it still made him feel uncomfortable all the same. He didn't know why, but her stare was just a little too pensive. Like she was considering something about him, but the problem was, she didn't know fuck all about him to know anything. Anything she thought were all conclusions she had drawn on her own, and he wasn't here for that shit.

"And this man—Nazio Donati, yes?—will also be living in the residence," the woman said.

"He owns the penthouse?" Roz's question came out slightly

sarcastic, and yet still annoyed at the same time. "He's also been my long-term boyfriend for over—"

"Not husband," the woman interjected.

Naz blinked.

Roz quieted.

"Because that could present a problem. The girl will need to be brought into a stable household. We consider that to be, more often than not when presented, a couple that has proven their—"

"The only reason she isn't my wife is because she has spent the last several years on an entirely different continent than me," Naz said sharply, "and I thought it wasn't appropriate to marry someone when we couldn't begin an actual marriage together in the same house, let alone country, but okay."

That made the woman clear her throat. Roz, to her benefit, shot Naz a small smile. This whole fucking charade was getting on his goddamn nerves, and Naz wasn't the type to let small things get to him like this, but here they were … doing exactly that.

From the paperwork … to the officials being in and out of his goddamn house, to this bitch trying to insinuate that their home wouldn't be an appropriate place for Penny to be fostered until she was eighteen, or something else came about that would mean she needed to be moved. It all just pissed him off spectacularly.

He never asked for this.

None of it.

But Penny didn't ask for her life to be the way it was, either. And Roz couldn't help that she had a heart of gold. Which meant Naz was going to do whatever he needed to do for Roz, including getting Penny under their roof.

The woman cleared her throat—frankly, Naz could have asked her to repeat her name, but she wasn't important enough for him to give a shit to know it. "All right, well, Rosalynn, I will get all of this filled out, and put into the system so we can … hopefully have Penny with you as soon as possible. From what I understand, she has asked to be allowed to live with you as well, and judges often consider older teenager's requests when needed."

"She … did?"

"I'm sorry?"

"Penny," Roz clarified, "she asked to live with me?"

"Apparently. Have a good day."

It was only once the woman was gone from their penthouse, and Naz had followed Roz into the kitchen where she could pick up the bottle of water, she'd discarded earlier did he finally speak to her.

"So, if they're going to push that line," he said, "we'll get married."

Roz, standing at the island with her back turned to him, spun around to face him with wide eyes. "What did you just say?"

"If they push the line about the fact we're not married or common law, then we can get married, Roz. It takes twenty-four hours after getting a marriage license to get married at the City Clerk's office. It's not a big deal."

"Not a—"

"No, it isn't," Naz said. "It's easily fixed. They won't fuck us around with her because of that, I assure you."

He'd make sure of it. Also, his family, and Roz's, had deep pockets and a lot of fucking contacts to use. Some money shoved into the right hands, and all these issues were going to go away, anyway.

A small smile played at the edges of Roz's lips. "So, you're telling me that despite the fact we haven't even told our parents that we're expecting a baby … or that we're bringing a sixteen-year-old girl into our home to live with us, we should get married and add that to the pile, too."

Well, when she put it like that …

Naz shrugged. "They would understand."

Or not.

It didn't matter.

"I don't think we'll need to do that," Roz said. "We are the best choice for her, and like Rebecca said, Penny did ask to live with me."

Yeah, Rebecca.

That was the bitch's name.

All right.

Naz filed that away for later. "So, does that mean you don't want to do that at all, then?"

Because that was really going to fuck up the plans he'd been working on from the moment he knew she was coming home to him—long before he even knew about the pregnancy, too. He'd scrap those plans if they needed to jump into marriage for the sake of Penny, but that was a different thing.

"What, get married?"

"Yeah, babe," Naz said, shrugging.

Roz gave him a look from the side. "You've never asked, Naz."

"Yet," he returned, "I have not asked yet."

His girl grinned. "Exactly."

Naz nodded at her water. "Take that prenatal vitamin, too, while you're at it. You didn't take it this morning."

She had so many things to think about, he was picking up the slack in other areas for her. He didn't mind, though. Wasn't that the whole point of loving someone? When they needed you, no matter what, you were there?

Because that's what Naz had been taught.

That's what he knew from his parents.

This was the only way he knew how to love Roz.

"Yeah, I will," she said, giving him a wink. "And what are you dressed up for?"

By dressed up, she meant the fact he'd shrugged on his leather jacket, and had his Doc Martens laced around the back, ready to go out.

"I need to meet up with Luca," he said. "Business stuff, you know."

Roz nodded. "Okay. And then dinner tomorrow at your parents with everybody, right?"

Naz grinned. "To share the news, yep."

He couldn't fucking wait.

She came across the kitchen, pushed up on her tiptoes, and pressed a sweet, lingering kiss to his lips. "I better call across the pond and see if Penny wants to talk today."

Naz swept his thumb across her cheek. "She'll talk for you."

Roz was literally the only person Penny cared to talk to on a personal level, now. Anything beyond giving a few words to police or her therapist, and Penny shut the fuck down. She also didn't have a problem meeting Naz's gaze on the few times they met, but she wouldn't say a single word to him.

Not even hi.

"Okay, go play with my brother," Roz said, patting him on his cheek.

Naz chuckled. "Play, right."

She could believe that.

He didn't mind letting her.

After all, the second Roz had told him about one of her last meetings with Penny before they left England where the girl explained a network of people were involved in this … thing that victimized Penny, well, time started ticking down.

Naz was about to really get started.

Some people just deserved to die.

Roz didn't need to know that, though.

For now.

ELEVEN

Naz

"Are you fucking serious?"

"If you're going to hover over my shoulder," Naz snapped at Luca, "then do us both a favor and fuck off somewhere."

"Naz, this is—"

"The only reason I came over to your place is because I couldn't very well get my system up and running without Roz watching me do it. I don't want her to worry about this. Got it?"

Luca paced behind Naz's chair as several PC screens came to life in front of him. On his lap, the laptop was already booted up and ready to take a trip onto the black web where he knew with a few clicks and the right keywords, he was going to find forums.

"Give me a username," Naz said.

Luca rolled his eyes and glared at the ceiling. "This is stupid."

"It isn't. And you're going to help me round them up."

Like pigs to the slaughter.

Naz didn't add that part out loud.

"Do you realize how large these networks are?" Luca asked. "They span continents, Naz. So what, you pick off a few of them here, and then what happens you come across a fucking video of some little kid in Asia somewhere being—"

Naz let out a sound that ached when it came out of him. "Then, the next time I am in Asia, I will take a side trip."

His friend cursed a blue streak under his breath. "You are inviting in trouble. If those fucks attention wasn't on you or us before, they will be now. Is that what you want—when you have kids, do you wanna go on the dark web and find pictures of them being distributed because they're a target? I hear two hearts inside each other, depending on the color stamped on the picture, means which gender they prefer. They're pretty cool with listing the ages of preference right beside it, too."

That made Naz hesitate as he found a forum called Little Dreams. Sickness welled in his gut because that was a lot more than he wanted to understand, but he had a feeling that wasn't even the tip of the goddamn iceberg. Once he went down this rabbit hole, there was going to be no coming back from it—a picture of a kid as a target would be the least disturbing thing, to be sure.

Did he really want that?

"And what happens when they figure it out?" Luca asked. "What happens when they start putting it together than the man in the forum is the one hunting them down?"

"I actually like the sound of that, so don't use it to discourage me."

They were animals.

He didn't mind hunting them like one.

"My point is, which you completely fucking missed, is that they'll go underground," Luca said.

"More than dark web forums and secret networks that even we don't know about?" Naz returned.

"Exactly, Naz."

"I hear what you're saying."

"Do you? Do you really? Because if you put me or mine in danger for this, I will gut you. Do you hear me?"

"I hear you."

And he understood that, too.

"Good. Make sure of it."

Luca turned to leave the secondary office space Naz had set up in his friend's home as a backup just in case, for some circumstance or another, he couldn't use the one in his own place. Naz spoke up to say one thing before Luca could leave entirely.

"Her father is a multi-billionaire," Naz said.

Luca hesitated. "What?"

"Penny. Her father is a billionaire from Jersey. Made his money through an investments company that worked overseas. You mean to tell me that some fuck from down the street on these forums have the kind of connections and money that man does to network like her father would? I bet ... I bet it's a layered thing, Luca. On the lower end, you've got people distributing the porn—videos, pictures, or whatever. And in the middle, you've got those who are a little better off, and maybe they have something to offer."

Naz twisted that word because saying what it really meant made him want to fucking puke. Still, he continued to drive the point home, adding, "They're the people the lower fucks who can afford it are going to, and the top tier? They're the ones using the middle of the spectrum when they find something specific ... and I wouldn't doubt for a second that they have their own—" Naz made another noise under his throat. "Like Penny ... like Penny, Luca."

"Naz, I get it's fucking horrifying, okay? I get it."

"No, you really don't. Do you know what she told Roz?"

"God, don't make me ask. I don't want—"

"Just because it is not in your home, affecting your life does not mean you have the right to ignore it happening to someone else."

Luca's gaze hardened as he looked back at Naz. "What did she tell Roz?"

"She was four—her virginity was auctioned off by her father. Three quarters of a million. She was flown to Hong Kong to deliver for the buyer. Four, Luca."

Luca was quiet for longer than Naz cared to admit. As his friend chewed on those words, and decided what he wanted to do with it, Naz turned back to the screen. Without warning, the username he wanted to use on the forum came to his mind, and before he could think better of it, he created an account.

At the doorway, Luca still hadn't moved to leave.

"You can't hunt them all down, it'll be impossible," Luca muttered.

Naz didn't need to be told, although it hurt his chest like nothing else. "I know."

"You're going to chase a rabbit hole, Naz."

"What if ..."

"What?"

"What if I made a program, Luca, that traced every picture, and every person in these forums. It'd have to be advanced ... crazy advanced, right? I can code it to run information through other databases."

"Hack databases, you mean," Luca countered.

Naz shrugged. "But I've done that before—I've been in government databases and back out with no one knowing I was even there. It's not impossible. I could do it again ... if I could match information from profiles or pictures to real kids with real parents or the people doing this to them ... it could be anonymously delivered to police across the globe. Everything is on the internet now. Everything has security cameras with facial recognition. I could make a fucking program—I could do it."

"A program like that, one that could actually grab information when everything from IPs to ... shit, everything and everyone on the dark web use proxy servers and VPNs, Naz. That's before the fail safes put into place by the people running the forums and ... You know it's not that easy, we use it for gunrunning."

"I know how they work, I made one, remember?"

A whole online, deep web network for the gun trafficking side of his father's business. Yeah, Naz knew how it worked.

"But nothing is perfect and all I need is the right program to get past those safe guards," Naz said. "I could do that—I could make it."

Luca made a noise under his breath. "... Fuck, Naz, that could take—"

"Years, I know." Naz frowned at the screen in front of him as he scrolled through a forum topic that described the grooming and sale of a child from Alabama. Holy fucking shit. "But I don't have years, Luca. I have nine months."

"What?"

"I have nine months before my baby is born. I don't have years to do this."

Because he couldn't imagine his child coming into the world when this was all around them. And if he didn't do something, then what good was he?

"Is Roz—"

"Dinner tomorrow," Naz interjected. "You should come and hear the news like everyone else."

"Shit."

"And these kids ... they don't have years, either. Once was one too many. I can't hunt them all, but I can get rid of a lot of them."

"Except they keep coming back," Luca replied, "it's not something you can eradicate like a diseased animal, or something. When these ones are gone, someone else will take their place. Just like with anything else. All you can do is protect your kids from it the best you can, Naz."

He didn't need the reminder, but he still had to do something. For now, he would settle on doing this until he figured something else out.

But the ones at the very top? Ones like Penny's father?

Naz would save those as a lesson—a lesson that would really hurt when he drove it home—for the rest that somehow managed to escape his notice. Someone was watching them, and someone was coming for them.

Every fucking one of them.

TWELVE

Naz

The chatter at the table continued despite the fact Roz had looked to Naz with an arched brow as if to silently ask, *Now*? He shrugged, letting the choice be up to her. They had spent the first hour of this family dinner explaining to the important people from both their families that a teenage girl would be living with them, and very little else. The whys weren't important, nor was it their business to share the things that Penny had gone through over the years. They answered as many questions as they were asked, but when it came right down to it, they said very little about it.

This was their choice.

Or rather, Roz's.

Naz was just here to let her do what she needed and wanted.

"Should I go get it, then?" Roz asked.

Naz grinned. "I will go get it. You should grab another plate of that lasagna your ma made. It was good."

"Because I need a second plate."

He was already standing from the chair, ignoring the curious gazes of their family that drifted his way when he did so. Dropping a kiss to the top of Roz's head, he said, "Who said anything about need, babe? It's all about what you want."

She grinned.

He winked.

"Where are you going?" his father called from the head of the table.

Naz passed his father a look as he headed for the entryway of the dining room. In his captain chair, Cross never looked happier to Naz. There was something about being surrounded by his entire family that made his father most happy. Well, his family and his friends, when it came to Roz's family. And they were all happy to finally have Roz back home, even if they were a tad bit worried about the new circumstances with Penny.

They might not have been voicing those concerns loudly—if only because they didn't want to say the wrong thing or step on someone's toes—but Naz could still tell. He wasn't stupid, but he appreciated his parents', and Roz's parents', effort to let them figure this shit out on their own. He didn't doubt for a second that once everyone knew the second piece of their news, that concern would ratchet up a bit.

Oh, well.

"I have something to grab in the car," Naz told his father.

"What?"

"Well, if we wanted you to know that when we first arrived, then you would have known, no?"

Cross smirked. "Oh, you're in that kind of mood today, huh?"

"Let the man go, Cross," Zeke said from across the table.

"Let me needle him. No one else does."

"Except he acts just like you, and we know where that leads."

"Did I ask—"

Okay, that was enough for Naz. Zeke and Cross were only joking around with each other, but they could continue to do that without him standing right there to listen to it. He had other, more important things, to be doing.

"I'll be back," Naz said as he slipped out of the dining room.

He heard his father shout after him, but he was already halfway down the hallway by then. Outside, their car was parked at the far end of the driveway because they arrived later than everyone else. A product of living in Manhattan when his parents still lived far outside the city limits. In the trunk of the car, Naz found the item they had kept hidden. Or rather, items. One was a cake Roz had decided to make, and despite the fact she wasn't exactly a baker, she had fun with it. It looked like it was going to make his teeth ache, too, what with the thick, white chocolate icing that looked like soft waves covering the cake, but apparently, she hadn't intended for it to be eaten at all.

The other two items, small, matching boxes with white bows keeping the tops firmly on were his idea ... just because. He ran around the city half of the evening the day before to find the things he needed to put inside those damn boxes when the cake probably would have been far more than enough, but hey.

His mother was a Marcello.

His father, a Donati.

They didn't go halfway.

They went all the way.

By the time Naz got back inside the house, the table had been mostly cleared but for a couple of bottles of wine that were being passed around. Roz passed on hers, but nobody seemed to think that was out of the ordinary. Naz took a glass for himself after setting the cake in the very middle of the table, and passing his mother one of the two boxes, as well as a box for Roz's mother, too.

"What's this?" his mother asked, passing a sly smile to Katya, Roz's mother. "Gifts, Naz?"

He chuckled. "Something like that."

Sitting back in his chair, he sipped on the bitter wine as he tossed his arm around Roz's shoulders. It was Italian tradition—rich, fatty, rich, fatty, sweet, rich, sweet, fatty ... that's how the meals went at an Italian's table. And then they always finished it off with something bitter to remind them of the sadness in life because the sadness was usually the most important. It was where the growth came. And it made them all the more grateful to be alive for it. Or, that's what his parents always explained.

Naz didn't know if it was true.

But he drank the bitter wine.

"And a cake?" Cross asked.

Naz waved a finger between the cake, and his father, as well as Zeke. "We thought while Ma and Katya opened their boxes, you and Zeke could ... cut the cake for us."

Zeke's brow dipped as he passed Naz a scowl. "Are you high? Who needs two people to cut a cake?"

Roz laughed. "Just do it. It's all in good fun, Daddy."

"Stop wasting time," Naz said, "cut the cake—and Ma, don't open that box until they're cutting."

"Why not?" Catherine said, her tone suspiciously whiney.

Naz only shook his head.

Nope.

They would find out soon enough.

Cross finished his wine with a huff and set the glass to the table as he gave his son a wag of his finger before lifting from his chair. That was another thing his father didn't like—standing from his chair before someone else at the table. He preferred to be the last person to leave a dinner, following right behind his wife.

That was just their way.

At the other side of the table, Zeke stood from his chair as well, but he kept a hold on the crystal glass with his remaining bit of wine. Two knives were picked up from the middle of the table, left over from dinner. As the two men popped the plastic cover from the cake holder, Catherine and Katya had their boxes ready to go.

It was only as two knives were cut through the cake did their mothers pull the bows from the boxes. It was timed almost perfectly—Catherine gasped first at the sight of two little gold crowns, one with pink gems embedded in the band, and one with blue, and Katya soon followed with a shout of happiness. The hollers from their fathers came right after as Cross and Zeke pulled two pieces of cake out with the knives, one with the middle colored in blue on one side, and one colored in pink.

Cross stared across to his son, a smile drifted over his face. "Another grandbaby?"

Naz nodded. "Yeah, Dad."

"Oh, Naz," Catherine whispered.

He shrugged.

Their pride was clear.

So was their love.

What else could he do?

Beside him, Zeke and Katya had already rounded the table with enough noise to break the windows to celebrate with them, too. A hand hit his back hard before Zeke bent down to hug his daughter. Kayta did the same. Under the table, Naz kept a hand on Roz's thigh because he knew this was probably a bit overwhelming.

"A baby," his father said again.

Naz laughed. "It's going to be a busy year."

"But a good one."

That, too.

THIRTEEN

Penny

Penny hated airports. Maybe it was the bad memories that she had locked away in the dark recesses of her mind that brought on those strong feelings whenever she as much as saw an airport sign, never mind being inside one, but she didn't like it. And knowing what was best for her mental health, she tried to avoid, as much as possible, anything that had her anxiety flaring.

Except she didn't have a choice today.

Avoiding the people flooding the corridor of the airport leading away from arrivals, she kept her head down. It was Penny's thing— no eye contact meant *no invitation to come near*. People liked to say she had permanent resting bitch face, and that was fine.

As long as it meant people left her the fuck alone.

What was the problem?

A man holding the hand of a toddler boy veered a bit too close to Penny as she walked by, and she had all she could do not to turn into a block of ice. The man hadn't given her a reason to feel that way, but that was the thing about the mind.

Muscle memory.

She'd been hurt by enough men that they all started to look the same from a distance. It was better for her *not* to trust them all, than to let even one in and be hurt again because she allowed one to become too close.

Right?

That was the story she was telling herself, anyway.

She was all too aware that it was a bit too hot for her to be wearing a long sleeve shirt, and black skinny jeans, but Penny didn't care. She ignored the stifling heat, and the way her clothes stuck to her skin. Black allowed her to blend into a crowd, and people were far less likely to notice the teenager with the sad, haunting face and the big, doll-like eyes when she kept her appearance muted.

No makeup. Her hair either down to cover her face or pulled back into a messy bun. Dark clothing all the way, and always long sleeves or pants to make sure no one would ever see the scars that covered her body from the cuts that allowed her to remember she could, in fact, feel *something*. Even if that something was nothing more than pain. Little to no jewelry. Even the messenger bag slung over her shoulder wasn't something that would draw attention.

That was all she cared about.

She didn't want people to *look*.

She didn't want them to see.

She didn't want to *be*.

Except here she was, in this fucking airport walking through arrivals at New York, because for some fucking reason, Penny was still here.

Being.

Alive.

She couldn't even kill herself right.

Fucking perfect, huh?

That was Penny's life in a nutshell.

• • •

"Where is your shadow today?"

Roz glanced over at her, and Penny did her best to meet the woman's gaze. The thing about Roz was that she didn't have to give a single shit about Penny, but for some reason, she did. And Penny really didn't know what to do with that, so she was *trying*.

She wasn't sure what she was trying for, or what it might mean in the end, but she still found herself doing it. That was why she asked to live with Roz when the officials called with paperwork to transfer her back to the States. It was the reason why, when it could have been the polite, sweet-natured female investigator who was handling her case asked if she wanted to be picked up by her at the airport, Penny still asked for Roz.

The woman cared.

For no reason.

They didn't even know each other.

She just did.

Penny was still trying to figure out what that fucking meant, and maybe that was the only thing about it that she didn't like. Which in itself was pretty strange because she didn't give a shit about anything anymore.

Weather?

Whatever.

Food?

Did she have to eat?

Life?

What was the fucking point?

But Roz …

She kind of liked Roz.

"Do you mean *Naz?*" Roz asked.

Penny sighed as their number was called, and the two of them approached the counter at the café Roz said they *had* to stop at before going home. "Yes, him."

She didn't know what to make of Nazio, either. He was quiet but *imposing.* Except he didn't impose himself on Penny, he was simply there. It was clear he cared a lot about Roz, and Penny liked *that.*

This was all very confusing for her.

"I asked that he stay at home," Roz said, "so I could pick you up, and we could chat for a bit before we go back to the penthouse together. Did you want him to come?"

Penny took a second to think about that. "I don't know."

Like most of her life.

"Can we get a decaf coffee, medium, and a hot chocolate, plus a dozen mixed pastries to go, please?"

The woman behind the counter nodded. "Absolutely. That'll just be a couple of minutes."

"No worries."

With her order in, Roz and Penny stepped to the side, allowing the person behind them to go up to the counter while they waited for theirs to be filled. Penny stayed quiet, unsure of what to say and not entirely sure about how she felt being back on American soil. It felt like she had been running for so long because at least that kept her away from home.

Away from pain.

Now, she was back.

Penny knew ... that pain would be coming soon, too.

Roz shot her a small smile. "Just for the record, if you feel uncomfortable with anything, Naz or otherwise ... all you have to do is say, okay?"

"Really?"

"Pardon?"

"All I have to do is tell you something bothers me?"

Roz shrugged. "Yeah. Why not?"

"Usually, when I told people something was wrong, they ignored me," Penny said, staring up at the chalkboard hanging overhead that described all the different drink options. "Or if I told someone that something they did was hurting me, they dismissed it as me being overdramatic, or worse, attention-seeking."

"That won't happen with us."

Penny glanced back at Roz.

She smiled back.

"Huh," Penny murmured.

"I'm sorry that's strange for you."

"I don't want people to feel sorry for me, Roz."

"What do you want, Penny?"

That was not an easy question.

Because … "I don't know."

"Let me know when you do, okay?" Roz turned a bit, facing the counter so that she would be ready when their order was finished. "Because that's all we're here to do—help you to get what you want, Penny."

Hmm.

"Oh," Roz added, glancing back at Penny, "that thing I wanted to talk about before we go home …"

"Yeah?"

"I'm pregnant, Penny."

For the first time in a long time, fear sliced through Penny's heart. She really wasn't sure *why*, or rather, she couldn't pinpoint exactly what caused the feeling. It was a mixture of things. Like the fact that every time she saw a young child, a part of her always wondered if someone was hurting that kid like people had done to her. Another part of her wondered if once the baby came along for Roz, would Penny have to leave to live with someone else?

"But the baby changes nothing," Roz said, "I just wanted to be the one to tell you."

"Oh, okay."

She was feeling something else, now.

Curiosity.

She'd never held a baby.

FOURTEEN

Penny

Four months later ...

"Wait," Penny muttered, stopping the DA from saying anything more about this *deal* they had settled out with her monster of a father and his horrible fucking lawyers. "Go back—so what you're saying is that he'll plead guilty to eighty-five counts of child pornography, right?"

"Yes," the man across the table said.

Underneath, where no one could see, Roz's hand squeezed tightly around Penny's. An ache had settled deep in her heart, because despite the fact she actually hadn't needed to see or speak to her father since this whole thing started ... every time she had to talk about him, or he was brought into a conversation, she felt ill.

She didn't want to think about him anymore.

He didn't deserve a space in her mind.

So, why was he still *there?*

Penny couldn't *cut* him out.

She tried.

"The deal says each count will have time served consecutively, and not together," the DA said, like Penny was a fucking idiot and needed it explained to her *again*. She heard it just fine the first fucking time. "With the maximum penalty for each charge, that could add up to over—"

"Just shut up," Penny said.

The man gave her a look. "Excuse me?"

"Penny," Roz said quietly beside her. "It's okay ... try to say what you're feeling, and not just try to hurt someone else because we're hurting, right?"

God.

Why did Roz have to be like ... *that?*

All the time, too.

"I think," came the dark voice of Naz behind Penny where he leaned against the wall of the kitchen in their *new*—because a baby needed lots of space, apparently—home, "what Penny is not quite saying but wants to, is that it's *just* the child porn charges, correct?"

"Yes, those are charges that will be impossible for them to win against."

"And nothing for her."

The man across the table stiffened. "Well—"

Naz didn't allow the man to continue on with whatever in the fuck he planned to say before he added, "So, perhaps you could forgive Penny that you made a deal with the man who raped her, and sold her body for years, wherein he will plead guilty to *everything* but what he did to her. Because you see, the only reason why you were able to get the child porn and charge him for that was because she came forward ... she talked, again and again and *again.* You put her on tape, you made her relive trauma to stranger after stranger. You put her in front of therapist after therapist to see if she was lying. You promised justice would be served for *her*."

"Sir—"

"And in fact," Naz continued, "what you did was use her to get what you could from him, and instead of getting her abuser on the stand to admit to what he did to her, she instead gets to feel like everything she did was not actually for her own benefit. So yeah, I think you could empathize with why she needs you to explain again why you made that choice. And without the attitude the second time around—go ahead, *try it*, Mr. Mahoney."

The DA swallowed hard and stared at the wood grain on the dining room table they currently sat at. Roz squeezed Penny's hand again, and she was eternally grateful for the support that she found in this house. It was strange to her in the way that those weren't at all the things she had been expecting when she came to live here with Naz and Roz.

Penny had become *so used* to being alone—to feeling numb to all and anything in her life—that now, it felt like she experienced too much when it came to her emotions, and she didn't know the first damn thing to do with them.

She was getting better, though.

One step at a time.

It was terrifying.

"Trial would be long," the DA murmured, "and drawn out. Media would be all over it—constantly. Penny would likely have to testify. No doubt in front of a packed courtroom, we'd be lucky if we were able to get a media ban approved by the judge, and certainly in full view of her father where he could stare at her while she retold detail after detail of his abuse. Which, again no doubt, would be for *his* pleasure, and certainly not for hers. So yes, I understand that on the surface, this deal doesn't exactly seem like it is to Penny's benefit—"

"Not one bit," Penny replied sharply.

"But your other options will be far more traumatic. He will die in prison, and it might not be because he *admitted* to the things he did to you, but it will be because of the strength and courage you have shown time and time again to make sure he couldn't do this to someone else."

Penny let out a shaky breath.

Why didn't that help?

Wordlessly, Penny stood from the table. Roz looked her way, a silent request for her to stay and finish this conversation reflecting back in the woman's eyes, but Penny couldn't. Right now, she just needed to be alone … or something.

Anything but this.

Roz always told her that was okay, too.

To be alone.

To need *time*.

It was okay, and she could take it.

As she headed out of the kitchen without as much as a look over her shoulder, Penny heard the DA say, "We don't need her agreement on the deal for it to go through, but I did want to let her know personally."

"Right," Naz snapped back, "because it is never about the victim, only the *victory.*"

"Or do you just have a personal problem with law enforcement, Nazio Donati, because of your *own* circumstances?"

"Get the fuck out of my house."

Penny heard the front door slam shut minutes later, but she was already at the back of the house, sitting in front of the baby grand piano that taunted her on a daily basis. For whatever reason, she hadn't been able to play it since she arrived in New York. It followed them from the penthouse, to the large, three-level home in the suburbs.

Roz played.

Naz did, occasionally, even if it wasn't *perfect.*

Penny, though?

Never.

Until right now. The urge thrummed deep, the notes taking shape in her mind the longer she stared at the glossy black smoothness of the piano legs.

Why now?

Why when she shouldn't care?

Why did it matter *now?*

Good girls play for Daddy, she heard him say in her head. *Oh, you missed a key, what does that mean?* And then, *Smile at the camera when you do that, Penny, they like it.*

"Fuck you, fuck you … *fuck you*," Penny mumbled, rocking forward on the bench. "Just … fuck you."

She pressed the heels of her palms to her burning eyes as she squeezed them shut, willing *his* voice out of her head, and for those memories to *burn*. Maybe that's what she had been looking for here, for this to take away all of that, but it was never going to go away.

Those memories would never leave.

It would never *not be*.

Her fingers trembled as she placed them to the ivory, the tune that came out of the instrument echoing and haunting through the halls of the quiet house as it matched the sounds she made when she cried.

And *God*.

She cried so hard.

The melody was so unlike what she had been known to play before—much darker, and deafening. A tune that had goosebumps racing over her skin and had her heart thumping hard against her ribcage.

It was pain.

Not pain she caused.

Not pain *he* made.

It didn't come from a razor against her skin, and it didn't hurt. It wasn't brought on by wrongs done to her, even if memories helped to create the music. It didn't leave scars behind, and it didn't linger long enough to make her wish she wasn't here at all.

It was pain put into music.

And it felt different like that.

Better like that.

For a long time, Penny had pushed music aside because it felt like a punishment. She had been put in front of a piano for her father's desire, not because anyone thought she would be any good at it. Her talents had then been used to please others, before they turned it around on her so that when she misbehaved, they punished her with it, too.

By sending her away *with* the music.

And she hated them.

Hated it.

But this was none of that.

This was all *her*.

FIFTEEN

Penny

Click, click, clack, click, clack, click, click.

Penny blinked, bleary-eyed and still tired, as she climbed down the dark stairwell of the suburban house where she had called home for the last several months Maybe it had been the trip to her therapist yesterday evening, but she'd had a train of nightmares since falling asleep, and she just wasn't in the mood to try again.

But what was that sound?

Penny found the source of the late-night noise soon enough. "What are you doing?"

The man on the couch stiffened, and just as quickly, shot a look over his shoulder at her. Reaching up, he was quick to close the laptop he'd been leaning over the coffee table to type on. "Nothing. What are you doing out of bed?"

"Can't sleep. Usually, when people say *nothing* they don't also feel the need to hide their computer screens, you know?"

Penny had a love-slash-hate relationship with the internet, and computers. She was like every sixteen-year-old girl who seemed to find too much self-worth on social media, and that was how she preferred to connect with people she wanted to keep in her life. It was easier than trying in real life because that always ended badly.

She had *no* friends in her new, private high school.

She had a few hundred on her socials.

It just didn't have to be deep.

But in the same breath, she *hated* the internet for many reasons. On certain places in the dark web, one could find folders upon folders of photos of her that were up for sale. Ranging from the age of one, up until she was almost thirteen. Those photos had not yet fallen into hands that could distribute them beyond the dark web where it would touch the people in her real life, but it all still felt a little too real to her.

And *raw*.

Sometimes, her life felt like a time bomb that was constantly ticking down. *Someday*—maybe—those photos would find their way out into the world. Penny wasn't fucking stupid, she knew how horrible people could be. They wouldn't care that she was a human trafficking victim. They wouldn't care that those photos were proof of her sexual abuse. All they would see, for the slightly older ones, were a young girl showing her body to a camera.

She hoped they *never* saw the light of day.

Naz sighed, and then chuckled. "Maybe you're not wrong, then, but that doesn't mean it's any of your business about what I was doing, either."

"Fair enough." Penny crossed around the couch and dropped into the recliner across from where Naz was sitting. "So, what are you hiding?"

"You think I would tell you?"

"Why not?"

"You know, I think this is the longest conversation we've had since you moved in with us months ago, Penny."

She had to think about it, but it didn't take her very long at all to realize that he wasn't exaggerating. She blinked, trying to pull something out of her zipped lips to say that would be appropriate. All she managed to settle on was, "I didn't know there was a *me* for a long time—I didn't have a voice to use."

Naz nodded. "I know, I didn't take it personally."

"You know I like you, right?"

He raised his brows. "Oh?"

Penny shrugged. "I haven't tried to ruin your life yet—that's good sign number one."

"That's not funny."

"And that doesn't make it less true, either."

Naz made a noise under his breath. "All right."

"Now that all the deflections are past us," Penny said with a smile and a wave of her hand between them, "what are you hiding?"

Because he was, she knew.

Penny just had that *sense*—she looked at people, and she could tell when they were lying, of it they were someone who might hurt her. Naz didn't fall into the *hurt* category. Like Roz, all he ever did was try to help her, but in his own way. Sometimes, that meant giving her space, and letting her figure out whatever she needed on her own time. She appreciated that more than he could possibly know.

Rarely did people leave her alone.

Naz sighed loudly. "You tell me."

Flipping open the laptop, he turned it around on the table so

Penny could see what was on the screen … which wasn't anything that made sense to her. A bunch of letters and numbers and symbols on a white screen, filling it from side to side.

It looked like … HTML?

But more.

"Is that code?" Penny asked.

"Good call," Naz returned.

"You write *code*?"

Naz lifted one shoulder like it wasn't a big thing. "I do a little bit of everything, it's how my brain focuses."

Right.

Over the last few months, Penny had heard more than one person refer to Naz as a literal genius. She had seen enough of his white boards filled with formulas that she didn't understand around their house to know he was smart.

He was also *more*.

He left early in the morning—drove a black car and wore a suit. Words like *family business* and *made man* were thrown around in low tones like Penny wouldn't be able to hear if they spoke quietly. Which was crap, because she did hear. And because she had access to the internet, she looked that shit up.

Apparently, Naz's family, and Roz's … well, they were criminals. Not the kind of criminals that hurt Penny, but criminals under the law, anyway. And they had been that way for a long time. Penny never asked about it, she didn't think the details of what the internet told her were mafia families that had reigned in New York for years were something she really needed to understand, but here she was.

"What's the code for?" Penny asked.

Naz sucked air through his teeth. "That's … a harder answer."

"Why?"

"Because."

"That's a non-answer."

Naz gave her a look. "I just don't think I should talk—"

"Is it about the mafia?"

He kept staring at her, expression unmovable. "And what do you know about that?"

"What I found on the internet."

"That shit lies."

"But does it really?"

Naz's cheek twitched. "Are we talking about this code or the fucking mafia?"

"You're not a very good liar, are you?"

"Not to people I care about, no."

Huh.

He cared about her.

Penny peeked at the screen. "Is it going to run something?"

"Yes, a program."

"That does what?"

"Crawls the dark web, the public internet, and government servers, so long as they don't detect it. It'll cross countries, it'll even break through the secure internet protections countries like China has that they use to monitor and control their citizens."

Penny's brow dipped. "But why?"

"That's the hard part."

"Why?"

Naz straightened and folded his hands over his knees as he stared at her. "You told Roz there was a network of people involved in the … thing your father was doing. Right?"

Penny swallowed hard. "So what?"

"When the police asked you for more information about that, you went quiet."

"Because look what they did with my father."

"Right," Naz said, "but there are still people out there, Penny … hurting kids."

"And?"

"This program is going to catch them—or at the very least, identify them, and then gather evidence of their business on the dark web, which will then be compiled into zipped, protected files before being delivered to whichever law enforcement is closest to their areas."

She blinked.

That sounded … "That's impossible."

"No, it isn't. I had a base program to work off—one that was made decades ago called *Thorn*. It crawled the dark web looking for child porn, which it would then try to match using facial recognition and other landmarks, should the photos include those, to real children. The problem was, that was a white hat system. It only worked *legally*. It didn't go over the line into the gray, or outright black, sides of hacking on the dark web. So, it had limitations. Mine does not, and since it will run constantly without me needing to touch it, and as I have it going through so many servers that it'll never be traced back to me. Or rather, it would take them a very long time to figure out it was me.

"This program will hack into government databases, into *school* databases. It will pull pictures of children from online yearbooks, and teachers from school websites. It will pull criminal records, and it will look into workers whose photos are on the internet. I have a friend who is also working with a guy that runs a program which hacks into every single security camera that runs on Wi-Fi, which means at some point, it will also be able to just—"

"Run through faces from the general public," Penny said faintly.

Naz nodded and pointed at the laptop. "That was the last bit of code needed. All I have to do now is hit that black button where it says RUN in the left-hand corner, and the system will be live in the dark web."

"Can't other people detect it, or—"

"Highly unlikely, given the way it was designed."

"Don't the people using the dark web have things to protect—"

"It's going to hack into those systems, too. It'll create small worm holes that will be virtually undetectable, which will suck in their coded information, before running through it to decode as much of it as it possibly can. That will leave the program with information of the people behind the forums."

Holy shit.

"I know it doesn't change what's already happened," Naz

murmured, "and it's not going to make your life better or easier to get through what's been done to you, Penny, but it's going to help someone else. It's going to save someone else. Nobody gets to change the past—we can only change the future."

"Yeah …"

"The code is finished. You can press the black button, if you'd like."

She stared at the screen for a while.

Naz waited her out.

Then, without warning, Penny leaned forward, and hit the RUN button. The screen blinked, the white background turning black as the words turned white and began to scroll. It was almost beautiful, really.

"I still wish *he* was dead," Penny muttered.

"I can make that happen, too."

Naz said it so flippantly.

That's how she knew he wasn't lying.

"But *would* you?" she asked quietly.

"You should watch the news more often," Naz said instead, "I hear you learn a lot from it."

What did that even mean?

He didn't give her the chance to ask.

"How many names of people do you know that can be tied to this ring your father was involved in?"

"Not many. I rarely got their names."

"But *some*," he pressed.

"A few," she whispered.

"Would you write them down for me?"

Penny glanced over at him. "Why?"

"Sometimes, we just don't get what we want from the law, Penny."

Well …

He wasn't wrong.

SIXTEEN

Naz

"No Penny today?"

Roz gave her gyno a smile from the side as Naz helped her onto the bed. At least in this office, she had the comfort of a cloth robe, and not one of those awful paper ones. He was glad she found a *new* doctor to handle this pregnancy, because he was two steps away from killing the last one who had also come highly recommended.

"Not today," Roz said, "she didn't want to miss classes—big test."

"Ah, I see. Well, let's check out the little one with the doppler, and hear what we can hear."

"He's been moving a lot," Roz muttered. "Especially at night."

"Could be a she," Naz added under his breath.

Roz gave him a look from the side. "It's a *he*."

On the other side of the bed, the doctor laughed. "What, did you decide not to learn the sex during the last ultrasound? I thought you wanted to find out, Roz."

"The tech couldn't see, and at the one before that, she wouldn't tell us because she *wasn't one-hundred percent sure*."

Really, Roz was being nice. The bitch at the clinic was in a mood and had mentioned more than once that she didn't think parents *should* know the sex of their babies before birth. It was her personal opinion that clouded her judgement that day because she forgot that she was a tech, and not the pregnant mother.

"Huh." The doctor had that conspiratorial glint in her eye, before she reached for the smaller version of the ultrasound machine that she kept in-office just in case. "Well, if we can see today, do we want to learn? You're seven months pregnant, Roz, so the baby is only going to get bigger. And it will be almost impossible to tell until birth. *If* I get lucky and can see today, we'll know."

She passed Naz a look.

Did they want to know?

"If you want to," Naz told Roz.

Her sweet smile lit up her face. "I kind of do."

"All right. Let's see if we can find out," he said to the doctor with a nod.

"After we get the regular stuff out of the way," the gyno replied. "We'll do the normal checkup first and go from there."

The normal checkup, which included measuring Roz's growing stomach—which made Naz *so fucking happy*—and checking the baby's heart beat with the doppler, before moving onto looking at the test notes for Roz's sugars and proteins, took about fifteen minutes.

"But your proteins are a little high in your urine," the doctor noted, "so we're going to move up to two appointments a week instead of waiting until your eighth month for that just to keep an eye on it. Just to be safe."

"Okay," Roz replied

Naz squeezed her hand, hearing the nerves in her voice. One of her greatest, and constant, fears with this pregnancy was that something would go wrong. Even if she didn't constantly voice her worries, he knew it was still there, making itself known in that beautiful mind of hers.

Anyone that Naz asked said that fear was pretty normal, all things considered. A first-time mother, and a first birth ... it went hand in hand, and there wasn't very much he could do to help except let her worry and reassure her when she would let him. So, that's exactly what he tried to do as often as he could.

Once the machine was on, the gel had been put on Roz's stomach, and the screen turned to swirls of black, gray, and white, Naz's attention was caught. So was Roz's, it seemed. Just like whenever they heard the baby's heartbeat on the doppler, they both went quiet, and felt a sense of relief flooding them.

He kept one eye on the screen, watching the different shapes of his baby take form and one eye on Roz at the same time. There was something about *knowing* she was pregnant with his child and giving him this amazing gift of life that just stunned him into silence every single time. Nothing could get better than this, he would swear it.

"Okay," the doctor murmured, "let's go a little higher, seems the baby has already turned themselves down, so no breech, Roz ... that's good news."

Roz laughed. "Great."

"But that's going to make it a little harder. Luckily, for now ... they're facing outward. You're going to want them to turn around, but they've got time to do that, and a little bit of room. Right now, we might be able to see ... let's just try ..."

The doctor grew quiet as the wand moved along the curve of Roz's stomach, moving higher until she was satisfied that she had gotten it where she wanted. Her hand came to rest on Roz's stomach, too, gloved fingers pushing lightly.

"Open those legs, little one," she said.

Naz had no idea what he was seeing on the screen, but as long as Roz was comfortable, and it didn't hurt the baby, then he didn't mind. Another twenty or so seconds passed before the doctor nodded, and smiled as she let go of Roz's stomach, reached over, and hit a button on the machine to capture what looked to be something of a screenshot.

"There," she said, pointing at a *very* distinct shape. "What do we see there?"

Naz chuckled. "Well …"

"Boy bits," Roz said, laughing.

"Yep, that's a penis. Congrats, guys, he's a boy."

A boy.

Roz looked up to Naz, and he grinned back.

She had been right.

Not that he was surprised.

She was always right.

Bending down, he pressed a quick kiss to her forehead, using his palm to smooth back her hair while she smiled.

"Love you," he told her.

Roz sighed happily. "Love you, too, Naz." Then, just as quickly she added, "You better call Cross, huh?"

"Yeah, I will after."

"*Naz.*"

He looked down at her.

Roz winked. "Call your dad."

Right.

Because she just knew.

Cross was the first person he wanted to tell, and she didn't need Naz to verbalize it to confirm it. He needed to tell his dad because their legacy continued on.

Another *principe*.

Another one like them.

A *boy*.

"And Penny, too," Roz said, "call her right after because she wanted to know, too."

Naz laughed and dropped a kiss to her grinning lips that time. "I will call *all the people*, Roz."

"You better."

SEVENTEEN

Naz

"I do hope you understand the trouble I could face for allowing something like this inside my prison," the Warden droned on.

Naz wasn't really listening. He was more interested in reading the plaques on the man's walls. Not because they held any real importance or even, told a story he was interested in, but because it was more fascinating than this conversation.

Welcome to his life in a nutshell.

"Are you listening to me?"

"Not particularly," Naz returned.

"Then, maybe it would be better if you left. I have better things to do than discuss something *illegal* with a man like you."

Ah.

There it was.

It didn't matter what kind of official someone was. A cop, detective, or a fucking prison warden. They all stunk like the same kind of shit at the end of the day, and Naz never forgot it. Simple as that.

Straightening to his full height, Naz turned on his heels slowly to face the man sitting behind the desk. A good sixty pounds overweight, with his hair beginning to thin at the hairline and around the crown of his head, with a line of perspiration dotting his forehead, Naz thought he fit his job description well.

A false king with a Napoleon complex.

Shocking.

"Or," Naz said, wagging a finger at the man with a smirk curving his lips, "we can go back to discussing how your bookie will recoup your debt to him. See, because I am more than willing to pay that off, if you only indulge me here. Otherwise, we're going to see how well you can do your job—if they even let you keep it—when you're missing three fingers."

The warden's face whitened.

Naz smiled.

"Should we keep talking, then?"

The man spluttered, his cheeks reddening in his anger before all the fight left from him all at once. It was almost biblical, really. These people liked to act as though they were better than Naz because they considered themselves firmly on the right side of the law.

Facts were facts, though.

Everybody had shit to clean.

Including the warden.

"I don't know how we're going to make this work," the man muttered. "What you're asking for is—"

"A meeting with a prisoner. *Private*, nothing more." Naz shrugged. "Anything else that happens won't be on my time while I'm here. I've paid a lot of money to make sure of that, no worries. I simply want the man to know what's going to happen *before* it happens."

"And if he acts out and puts himself in isolation?"

"You'll make sure he stays in general pop."

The man cleared his throat, leaning back on an old office chair that creaked with the movements of his heavy body. He stared at the wall, avoiding Naz's stare at all costs. He wasn't even offended. It was hard to handle being blackmailed.

Not that Naz would know anything about that.

He was always on *this* side of the arrangement.

His father made sure he knew that.

"If I have a mess to clean because of your ... *meeting*," the warden warned.

Naz chuckled. "You'll *what?*"

"Well—"

"Nothing, I imagine. You'll do nothing. He's a child rapist. He's lucky to have made it this long in general pop. I suspect that's because guards are watching his back, but that's about to change, isn't it? As for this meeting, whenever you get the time set up, you have my phone number to give me a call. I can be here in a couple of hours."

The warden sighed, clearly giving up his fight.

Blackmail was a fun game.

Naz should play it more often.

"I will give you a call," the man muttered.

"Thank you."

· · ·

A week passed before Naz was back at the prison, only this time, he didn't see the warden at all. In fact, a guard was the one to greet him at the entrance before guiding him through the walls of the prison. He wasn't even taken through security—a sure no-no, he was positive.

Not that he minded.

"The wait shouldn't be too long," the guard said outside the doorway of what looked to be a forgotten office space. "He believes he's coming in for a chat with his lawyer. There is no video or recording devices in the room, and you will have fifteen minutes with him before someone will come to the door."

Naz grinned. "I only need five."

"So be it."

Naz entered the office space, closing the door behind him before he took the chance to look around. There wasn't much to see. Gray walls with lines of cracking paint. A few old prison policy papers taped to the cement. Behind the desk, a row of encyclopedias stood with spines out, forgotten. Overhead, bare bulbs provided the light for the room. A floor with a rug that could be replaced and looked older than his twenty-five years. He brushed a hand along the top of the standard-sized desk to remove the thin layer of dust, not bothering to move behind it to sit in the chair.

He didn't need the chair.

Naz perched himself on the left corner of the edge of the desk, stared at the door on the other side of the room, and waited. Thankfully, the guard hadn't lied, and he didn't have to wait very long before the doorknob jiggled, and a shackled man was shoved through the door before it was closed just as quickly behind him.

Preston Dunsworth.

Penny's father.

Naz smiled coolly when the man's gaze swung around and landed on him. He let the guy run through his gamut of emotions, the shock of realizing, no, his lawyer wasn't here like he thought he was.

"Who the fuck are you?"

Bold, you know, for a man wearing a prison uniform.

Naz shrugged. "No one important."

Preston's thick brows knotted together. "Important enough to be here. *Who are you?*"

"Do you often find when you make demands, that other people just … blindly follow along?"

The man didn't reply.

Naz didn't need him to.

He did take a moment to absorb Preston. He was a good six-foot tall, handsome by society's standards, and looked fit, even under the loose, drab uniform. Money, status, and privilege could buy a lot of things, and in this man's case, it had bought people's silence, and his own disgusting network of children to abuse. One wouldn't look at Preston and think *child rapist*. Everyone had a picture in their mind of what *those* kinds of people were, and this man didn't look like it at all. Naz was sure if they put him in a suit, splashed his face on the front page of a newspaper with a headline about charity, women would *swoon*.

They'd have no idea what he did.

What he *would* do.

What he had already done.

"Who are—"

"I am Nazio Donati," Naz interjected. "My grandfathers are Calisto Donati, and Dante Marcello. My father, Cross Donati."

The man's eyes narrowed briefly before they widened slightly with recognition. Yeah, in New York, or even New Jersey where this piece of shit hailed from, it was hard to miss a name like Donati or Marcello.

Naz nodded. "Yeah, I come from some of the most infamous Cosa Nostra bosses to have ever controlled the state of New York. And *me?* Oh, I'm just some genius with too much time on his hands, a massive bank account, and a goal, Preston."

The man swallowed hard. "What does the mafia want with me?"

"It's not the mafia you have to worry about."

"I—"

"One other thing about me," Naz said, pushing off the edge of the desk to stand. He fixed his jacket and brushed off any remaining dust from his pants. "I am the man who fosters Penny—the child you raped for years."

Preston took a huge step back.

Naz chuckled.

"That's pointless," Naz said, "and I promised I wouldn't make a mess here today."

"What do you wa—"

"Just to let you know some things, that's all. See, up until now, your life in prison has been pretty easy. Usually, general pop is hard on bastards like you, as it should be, but someone must be paying the guards on your behalf to keep an eye on you, right? *Shit*, you don't even have a bunkmate in your cell."

Preston turned to beat his hands against the window of the door. The idiot didn't even check the knob because if he had, he would have realized it was unlocked. Naz only laughed.

"They're not coming," he said, "I have fifteen minutes one way or the other."

Preston glared over his shoulder. "I don't know what you want, but you won't get anything from me."

"That's the thing. I don't need anything from you. I just wanted you to see us coming—*me*, really. If you make it to the end of the week alive, you'll be lucky, but I bet you won't make it further than that. While you're in here, information is being distributed to the prisoners. Every single one of them will know what you did, and who you are. I'm sure you've seen how other rapists get treated once the rest of general pop knows. You've got shower time tonight, right? Don't fight too hard when they rape you—I hear you'll bleed less."

Preston's face whitened.

Naz smiled as he strolled across the room and grabbed the door before pulling it open. Giving the man a look from the side, he shrugged. "And just to make sure you don't make it to the end of the week here, there's a bounty on you now. And believe it not, I didn't have to pay very much for that because you're not worth *shit*."

"Go to hell, you piece of—"

He *had* promised this would be clean.

Instead, he left a bloodstain on the floor under Preston's bruised face when he reared back and broke the man's nose with a punch.

"That's from Penny," Naz said. "Everything else? That's *for* her."

And the man deserved everything that was coming for him.

EIGHTEEN

Penny

"Miss Dunsworth, what is the square root of—"

"Pass," Penny muttered.

"You can't just pass a question because you don't want to answer it, Penny."

She sighed. "Pass."

Light laughter filtered through the classroom, but Penny was more interested in staring out the window. She would much rather do her studies online, or even with a tutor at home, but the chick who came around every once in a while to check in on Penny, and her living situation being fostered with Roz and Naz said it would be better for her to be *in* school.

With people.

Yuck.

The only good thing about this hell was the fact that Roz had allowed Penny to pick what school she wanted to attend, and then Naz came in to drop a whole bunch of money to make sure Penny had just enough freedom to breathe here.

Like now.

Sticking her hand up, the teacher's gaze drifted to her. "Yes?"

"I want to go see Mrs. Canns."

The school counselor.

The teacher's lips pursed like she was considering refusing Penny's request, but the woman eventually nodded with a jerk of her thumb toward the door. It took Penny no time at all to pack up her shit, and head out of the classroom, leaving the rest of the teenaged idiots behind her. She was only here because she needed to be—she needed a fucking *diploma*.

That was it.

She didn't have friends.

Didn't want them.

No one here would ever understand Penny, or her life. She was the weird one—the *freak*. In gym, they noticed she only wore long sleeve shirts, and black leggings. And so, the rumors about what she was hiding under her clothes started. Not that they were wrong, she just didn't care to indulge them. The group of High Bitches in Charge and their merry band of fucktoys for boys made it their mission to piss Penny off at least once a day, and that was a feat.

You know, considering Penny felt nothing.

Most of the time.

She didn't go to the counselor. Instead, she headed outside through an exit door, and pulled a small metal case from her bag. Flipping it open, she found a handful of cigarettes, and two joints. She'd save the weed for later ... *maybe*.

Roz didn't like it.

Naz didn't have an opinion.

It soothed her mind.

It was the only time she didn't have to *think*.

Lighting up a cigarette, Penny let the smoke soak into her lungs as she stared out over the west side of the parking lot. No doubt, the school already had her on camera coming out to smoke, and someone was on their way to drag her back inside. Security, likely.

She didn't want to go back in there.

She didn't want to be here at all.

And not just *here* … but here.

Alive.

Breathing.

On earth.

That was when Penny realized her depression was back, and better than ever. It wasn't like it had gone away, really, but it became far more manageable over the last year. She didn't know what it was like to live without depression. At three years old, she had her first moment of suicidal ideation. Here she was at seventeen, and she was still looking out at the road thinking … *how easy would it be to just run out in front of traffic?*

Fucking bitch.

Yeah, that's exactly what depression was.

A goddamn bitch.

"Penny Dunsworth, get back inside the school right now!"

Penny sighed.

Figures.

She didn't do as the security guard told her. Instead, she stood, slinging her messenger bag and purse over her shoulder before she darted into the parking lot without a look over her shoulder. She didn't have a car here—still didn't know how to drive.

Not that it mattered.

She didn't mind a walk.

Penny just didn't know what she was walking toward anymore.

• • •

"Do you ever work?"

Naz didn't look the least bit surprised to see Penny standing in the doorway of their living room. "Do you ever stay at school like you're supposed to?"

"Bad day."

"Idiots again, or …?"

Penny shrugged. "Bad thoughts."

That was her way of *letting them know* without saying something about her depression. She kind of felt like it was a check on herself, in a way. If other people knew she was having dark thoughts, she was less likely to act on them with self-harm, or something of a similar nature. It didn't always work, but it helped.

Especially with Naz and Roz.

They didn't judge.

Naz folded his arms behind his head and eyed her from the side. "I do work, actually. And do you know what else I do?"

"Not particularly."

"Get phone calls from the school when you skip out. I figured you would be coming home, so I said I would be there to meet you. I should be on the other side of the city, though."

Huh.

"Where's Roz?"

"You have to stop skipping school."

"I would if I could do it online."

Naz lifted a brow. "You're supposed to *socialize*. It's a good thing to learn."

"I do. With you, Roz, and people around here. That school is annoying."

"Is it, or is it—"

"I hate that school, and the people in it."

"You chose that school."

Penny rolled her eyes so hard it hurt. "Because I *had* to."

Naz pursed his lips. "Two days at the school, three days at home online."

"Oh, we're bartering now?"

"Everybody gets something they want."

"What will the social worker say?"

"Fuck her," Naz said, "her shit doesn't work, anyway."

Well …

He wasn't wrong.

"Two days there, three here," she agreed.

Naz nodded, clearly pleased. "You only have a few months left to go before you graduate. At least try to make it until then."

"Yeah, but then what happens?"

He was silent.

Penny, too.

"Well," he finally said quietly, "that's the beauty of it, Roz. You can do whatever you want."

But could she?

Could she *really*?

"I don't ... know what I want," she admitted.

Naz gave her another look from the side. "Yeah, I imagine that's a big part of the problem, huh?"

More than he knew.

Penny didn't understand her purpose.

Why was she even alive?

"And you didn't answer me—where is Roz?"

"Getting a massage right about now. She worries all the time. About the baby, me ... *you*. She rarely even takes time to play the piano lately. So, I set up a day for her to relax, and nothing more. Which is why I am here right now, and she is not."

"Are we going to tell her I skipped again?"

Naz scowled. "Probably not."

"I'll try to do better."

She expected a *but will you?*

Instead, he smiled. "The best you can do is all we ask for, Penny."

Yeah, she knew.

It's why she was still here.

That, and ... "Did you guys pick a name yet?"

"We were thinking Cross, for my father."

"I like it."

"Roz is going to ask you to be a godmother."

Well, then.

Penny just blinked.

Naz said nothing as he pushed up from the couch until he came to stand in front of her. "And I thought you would like to know, before someone calls and tells you."

"Know what?"

"Yesterday, your father was found murdered in the prison kitchen. Apparently, he washed dishes to earn privileges. They're not really sure what happened ... but dental records confirmed the identity this morning."

Penny stilled. Naz let her have the moment.

She almost wanted to ask if he did it. But *how?*

He'd said he could make it happen, after all.

A part of her wanted to have a breakdown right then and there. Her fragile mental state could never be trusted to handle something like this. Another part of her felt a sick sort of glee to know one of her monsters—the biggest of her demons—was dead. The rest of her felt nothing at all, but that wasn't unusual.

An old friend, really.

Penny decided to ask, "Do you think God forgave him for what he did to me?"

Naz considered that. "I don't know."

"Well, I never will."

"I'm sure he died knowing that."

Good.

It's what he deserved.

NINETEEN

Roz

"I can't wait to meet you, little man."

Roz smiled, the sleepiness drifting away from her mind as she listened to Naz murmur to their unborn child. She swore the baby could hear his father perfectly fine, too, and *knew* it was his dad talking to him because he suddenly became far more active than he usually was first thing in the morning.

The graze of his warm, calloused fingertips drifting across the expanse of her stomach had Roz finally opening her eyes. Sunlight spilled in from the bedroom window, making streaks across the gray sheets on their bed. She had the *perfect* view of Naz in his mostly naked glory, laying sideways on the bed so he could talk to her stomach.

God.

She loved him more.

It just kept growing.

"One more week," he said to the baby.

"Or more," she said tiredly.

Naz's gaze lifted sheepishly over the blankets to meet hers. "Did I wake you up?"

Roz shrugged. "It's okay. This was a nice thing to see first thing in the morning."

"Oh?"

"More than you know."

Naz put his palms to Roz's swell where her over-sized tee had ridden up throughout the night to press a kiss to her skin. Just like that, the unborn baby boy calmed, and she dragged in a calming breath.

Thirty-nine weeks pregnant today.

And it was her baby shower.

"Is Penny awake?" she asked.

Naz hummed under his breath. "Don't know, haven't left the bedroom."

"How long have you been talking to the baby?"

He wouldn't meet her gaze.

"Naz?"

"Not long, like an hour."

An hour.

Her heart swelled.

"You are the cutest thing," she told him.

Naz sighed and stared at her over the crest of her stomach. "Glad I can amuse you. Now," he said, pushing up from his elbows so that he could hover over her slightly. He dropped a kiss to her lips, soft, slow, and teasing, before murmuring, "… what can I do for you, hmm?"

"What does that mean?"

"You seem to think I'm *cute* … which means I need to remind you what I really am."

Oh, she didn't need to be reminded.

She knew very well.

Roz wasn't about to refuse his suggestion, though.

Grinning, she said, "You better hurry up and show me before I forget, Naz."

• • •

Roz ignored the slight twinge in her back, more caught up in the flying confetti that filled the room from confetti cannons. Blue, silver, and gold confetti danced high in the air before it covered the floor. The shouts from her family, and Naz's, had her smiling wider than ever as the large blue and white cake was pushed in from the entryway of the mansion's ballroom. It was five layers high, and *amazing.*

"Oh, wow," Roz said.

Her mother laughed at her side. "Isn't it beautiful?"

"Excessive."

"*Well,* we never do things half way."

That was fact.

"Okay," Catherine called out, "cake first, gifts second!"

Roz was only half listening. "Where's Penny?"

Katya peered around. "I don't know. I can send Naz out to look for her, if you want."

Well …

"Maybe she needed a breather," Roz said, "there's a lot of people here tonight."

Sometimes, that happened with Penny.

Roz didn't fault her for it.

"If you're sure," Katya said.

"Yeah, let's cut the cake."

Naz was already there, knife in hand and a big smile firmly in place. Not that it was shocking—his sweet tooth was widely known.

"How big of a piece do you want, hmm?" he asked her. "You get the first one."

Roz's smile slipped when that twinge came back in her back. Naz didn't miss it.

"You all right?"

She waved it off. "Long day on my feet."

This baby shower was *way more* than she asked for. The pile of presents on the large table nearly reached the ceiling, and that wasn't an exaggeration.

God knew she was grateful, though.

"Naz will cut your piece," Catherine said, coming up to press a quick kiss to her son's temple, "and we will find you a seat to relax for the rest of the party. How's that?"

"Sounds perfect."

• • •

"There you are."

Penny glanced up from where she sat on the back steps of the mansion. After eating the cake and spending three hours opening gifts—Naz had to step in to help—Roz realized Penny was still nowhere to be seen. So, when she had the chance, she slipped out to go in search for the seventeen-year-old.

She found her.

"Sorry," Penny said, her grip on the gift box tightening, "I just … so many people wanted to talk to me, I couldn't get a break."

Roz smiled before making her way over to sit beside Penny. "You know that's not a bad thing, right? The fact they make an effort to talk to you, and spend time with you, I mean. It means they care."

"I know."

"Still overwhelming, though?"

Penny shrugged. "I'm not good with people, that's all."

Roz bumped the girl's shoulder with her own. "It'll take time, and they don't mind waiting."

Penny was worth it, after all.

"What's that?" she asked, pointing at the gift box.

"Oh, the baby's present."

"The *baby's*?"

"Well, you have everything you want. And I wanted to get the baby something special. Not just … clothes or toys. Something important."

Roz's heart swelled.

"Really?"

Penny smiled. "Yeah, I mean, it's not much, but—"

"Whatever it is, it's perfect."

Because it came from Penny, and the girl cared enough to do

something for someone else, but especially Roz. That meant the world to her. All she wanted was for this young woman to find her place in the world and get *healthy*. To love life and find a reason to keep living for it.

The gift was a small thing.

Insignificant to others.

Everything to Roz, though.

"Want to open it?" Penny asked.

Roz sniffed back the tears—stupid hormones—and reached for the box. She carefully untied the silk ribbon on the top and lifted the lid from the box. There, resting inside white tissue, was a brown teddy bear with a blue ribbon around his neck.

"Press his hand," Penny said.

Roz did.

Music filtered from the bear.

Soft, and calming.

A song she never heard before.

The *piano*.

"Is that yours?"

Penny nodded. "I wrote it for the baby, and had it recorded to go inside the bear. It's about ten minutes long, so I thought maybe it would help to put him to sleep."

"Oh, Penny. That's beautiful."

So much more than just beautiful, really.

"It's perfect," Roz told her.

"You really like it? I know it's not something like what they gave you or—"

Before the girl could continue, Roz leaned over and took Penny into her embrace. She hugged the girl until Penny hugged back.

"It is *perfect*," Roz said, "the best gift you could have given the baby. Don't think differently."

"Okay."

Then, that small twinge of pain returned in Roz's back, only this time it was sharper, and lasted longer. She stiffened, a small groan leaving her lips before Penny gave her an odd look. She felt the warm rush of wetness between her thighs.

And all Roz could think of was *of course.*

"What's wrong?" Penny asked.

"Could you go find Naz for me?"

"Why?"

"My water just broke."

TWENTY

Roz

"Calm down," she murmured, trying to keep her tone calm lest she make Naz panic *more*. Was that possible? She didn't think so, because from the very second Naz knew she had gone into labor, it was like all those smart cells in his brain just disappeared. "You're going twenty over the limit, Naz, and I don't even need to go to the hospital yet."

"You're in labor—*yes*, you need to go to the hospital."

"How many books did you read on pregnancy and birth?"

"A lot."

He didn't even look over at her in the passenger seat as he spoke, simply kept his gaze on the road as he swerved in and out of traffic. That alone was going to give Roz a fucking heart attack.

"And what did the books say about a first birth?"

Fuck.

She could feel the tightening starting in her lower back again. The telltale sign of an oncoming contraction. They were still seven to eight minutes apart, and only two to three minutes long each time. Not that it made a difference, because while it was *early* … and she undoubtedly had hours of this to go yet, it still hurt like hell.

God.

"That it would take time, but—"

"Hours, it said hours. Days, in some cases."

"Your water broke."

Roz nodded, wetting the line of her lips, and hoping she could get her next few words out before she ended up right in the thick of a fucking contraction that would silence her for minutes while she tried to breathe through it. People and her birthing classes *lied*. Every single one of them. They said it was like a wave—the contraction came in slow, like water climbing up the shore like, and then it became stronger and stronger until it reached its peak, before rushing back out, and giving her relief.

She found it just fucking hurt.

The whole time.

The same intensity.

"They're going to send me home to labor," she said, teeth starting to clench, "and you know it."

"But—"

"And then it'll be an hour to drive home, and another hour to drive back to the hospital."

"Roz."

"Yeah?"

"Babe, you just had three contractions in the span of fifteen minutes."

She blinked, staring over at him from the side as that pain sharpened and made her vision blurry. Focusing on the breathing technique which was *supposed* to help with the severity of the pain, it made it difficult to see Naz, and speak to him at the same time.

"I've been timing it," he added quieter.

Right.

She had, too.

Somehow, she must have fucked up.

"So about three minutes apart," he said, "and two minutes in between ... which means yeah, we need to go to the hospital. *Now.*"

Yeah.

She got that.

Now, it was her who was panicking. It hit all at once that there was no going back at this point. Up until that moment, pregnancy had just been ... *pregnancy.* She didn't worry too much about birth because she had never experienced it, and she wasn't sure how she would react once she was in the thick of it.

Well, now she knew.

It hurt.

She didn't like it.

And it was only going to get worse.

"Where's my mom?"

"On her way with your dad, babe."

Roz attempted something akin to a nod, but she wasn't even sure if she actually did it, or not. *Perfect.* Just great.

"I'm not ready," she muttered.

"Little late, Roz."

Yep.

• • •

Naz

"Hello."

Naz's heart?

Too full.

His lungs?

Frozen.

A hazy-eyed baby boy squinted up from his arms, wrapped in a hospital-issue blanket. With a blue cap pulled over the wild mess of black hair, only a few tufts now stuck out around the edges. A tiny hand curled around the edge of the blanket, and *Jesus Christ* ... he was so small.

Not by *healthy* standards, or anything. He weighed eight pounds, seven ounces. He was a big, healthy boy.

And he was small in his father's arms.

Naz couldn't stop staring.

"Look at your little nose," Naz said, letting the tip of his finger trace the slope of his child's face. He was *perfect.* Every single inch of him, from the very tips of his ten toes—Naz counted—to the top of his head. "Can you see me, too?"

Probably not.

Babies didn't have good vision for a period of time after birth. It would take months before his child would be able to see him from across the room. And *still* ... when his boy opened his cloudy dark eyes and stared upward, Naz was sure they were seeing each other.

He felt that.

"Hey, little man."

Standing in the corner of the hospital room, one might think Naz was just getting to see his son for the first time. That would be the wrong assumption. In fact, Roz had been in labor for another eight hours *after* they arrived at the hospital with her being just four centimeters dilated. One centimeter too much for them to send her home, even though her contractions suggested she was farther along in the process than she was.

This child of his hadn't come into the world until closer to three in the morning. His family, and hers, slept in a waiting room down the hall, only waking up when Roz's mom went down to let them know the baby was born, but given the time, and the fact that Roz *needed* to rest because those last couple of hours had been hard—they still hadn't taken the baby out to introduce him to anyone.

Now, Roz was just waking up after a few hours of sleep.

Naz walked the floor with the baby.

He couldn't sleep.

Adrenaline too high.

Love, *too fucking much*.

"Have you put him down once?" he heard her ask.

Naz shook his head. "He doesn't know what that feels like—all he knows is what it's like to be cradled, and warm."

Her sweet hum of agreement had him turning to face her. Tucked under crisp hospital blankets, she finally looked *awake*, and good. Not the pain she had been in, or the exhaustion that hit her like a ton of bricks shortly after birth.

Slipping an item out of his pocket when Roz was distracted by the nurse who came in with a cup of water, a straw, and the promise of food as soon as she was feeling up to eating, of course. His son decided to play along with Naz's trick, although really, the baby seemed willing to grab onto anything that was placed in his palm or on his fingers. A natural reflex of infants, he knew.

"So, have we picked a name for the little guy?" the nurse asked.

Roz looked Naz's way. "Well?"

"I think we did."

A long time ago.

"Cross Zeke Donati."

"Very different," the nurse said, doing a quick check of Roz's vitals. "And you're looking well, so whenever you're ready to eat, we'll do that, and get you into a shower. Sound good?"

"Thank you."

Once the nurse was gone, Roz's attention turned on Naz, and the baby. "Bring him to me, let me see if he wants to eat."

"He *was* rooting."

"Mmhmm."

Naz grinned, keeping his hand over the baby's to hide the item now hanging on little Cross's index finger. Still blinking and trying to focus, the baby seemed happy to move from his father's arms, to his mother's. As though he could just *smell* her, and he knew who she was, his little eyes fluttered closed, and he turned his face into her chest.

Roz, readying to move her gown aside, and feed the baby, he knew the *second* her gaze landed on the engagement ring the baby held. Her sweet gasp, and the widening of her eyes had him grinning when her stare lifted to meet his.

Naz shrugged. "I couldn't find the right time to ask—the last few months were just busy ... and I didn't wanna take your attention away from planning for him, or from Penny, and—"

"*Yes.*"

"I didn't even ask yet."

"You don't have to, my answer is *yes*, Naz."

"You have to let me ask."

Her laughter colored the room, making the baby startle in her arms, although he didn't seem to mind. Leaning down over the bed, he pressed a kiss to her lips, feeling her smile curving against his own as he murmured, "Marry me, Roz?"

"Yes."

TWENTY-ONE

Naz

"Where's Dad?"

Katya shook her head, smiling. "Down the hall with Cross … someone—your father, but I'm not naming names, Naz—thought it might be unfair that Zeke saw the baby first. He was joking, mind, but Zeke took it seriously. He didn't think it would be fair for him to see the baby first without Cross. They decided to wait."

Naz, entirely unsurprised at that statement, laughed. That was his father, and the man's best friend in a nutshell. He often wondered how Cross and Zeke felt that, after decades of being best friends, they had kids that ended up together, not to mention, giving them a grandbaby, now. "At least they work out their nonsense without involving anyone else."

His fiancée's mother pointed a finger at him, her rare smartass coming out to play. "And that is the only thing that saves them from one of us killing them in their sleep—we don't tell them that, though."

She wasn't wrong.

He turned to Roz, who was slowly letting her mother help to get her dressed. Not that she was getting done up or anything. Comfy sweats, an oversized t-shirt, and a satin robe she had packed for after the birth. A shower and food had done wonders for Roz's tiredness, and let her throw her hair up, before she convinced her mother it would be just fine if she didn't go right back to sleep.

She could use a bit more rest, but she was determined to make the trip down the hall to the family waiting area so they could introduce the baby to *everyone* waiting. And it was a lot of people. They had big families.

It would be easier to do it all at once than a couple at a time coming in and out of the hospital room. At least then, Roz would be able to do this big one, and come back to sleep. She wouldn't keep getting woken up. She said she didn't mind, but ... well, it was time for her to relax. Simple as that.

Her mother's idea.

Naz agreed.

"You carry him down, okay?" Roz asked.

Naz nodded, smart enough to know he shouldn't say he was planning to do that anyway. He couldn't help it, really. Every single time he thought about putting his son down, something *hurt* in his chest, and he would just rather not. Besides, what did it matter? The baby boy liked to be held, and Naz liked to hold him.

Seemed simple to him.

An obvious answer.

Little Cross currently slept happily in his tight swaddle, a knit hat on his head to keep his ears warm, tucked in his father's arms. He would sleep fine in Roz's arms, too, but the second they tried to put him in the hospital-issued bassinet, he cried. And Naz swore all he heard when his son cried was *fear*. He wasn't sure if that was normal or not, but he couldn't stand to listen to the baby cry for them.

So fine.

He didn't have to be put down.

You'll spoil him, an older nurse had said. *Teach him he'll never have to sleep alone, and you'll never have a bed to yourself again, young man.*

Naz literally looked at the woman and asked, "*And?*"

She hadn't liked that response.

Was he supposed to care?

Soon, the three headed out of the hospital room. Katya on one side of Roz, and Naz on the other, with his arm tucked around her waist, and the baby safely sleeping on the other side. She rested her head against him, watching the baby with a happy, pleased smile.

He took just enough of both their features—a perfect mix, really—and it was hard not to stare, and admire. They *made* him—he was theirs.

Naz was still thinking about that when they strolled into the family waiting room. All the chatter instantly quieted, and he swore he felt a half a dozen gazes turn on them. His parents, Roz's father, their aunts and uncles—some who had come in from out of state just to see the baby. His grandparents, although hers had passed on a while ago, he suspected they were still looking out for them from above.

"*Look at him.*"

Naz grinned at his ma. "He's perfect."

And just like that, they were surrounded by people—their *family*. His father's hands found his shoulders, squeezing in congratulations as he peered down at the baby with pride.

"God, he's perfect," Cross said.

Zeke laughed, stepping in beside his best friend to get a look at his grandson, as well. "Definitely worth saving your ass for all those years ago, Cross."

"Watch it."

"So, did we go with what you wanted for a name?" his mother asked.

Katya nodded. "They did."

"Cross Zeke Donati."

"And we differentiate how?" his grandfather asked.

Naz shrugged. "We'll figure that out."

The baby was passed from his arms, to his mother's. It gave Naz a moment to talk to his grandmother, who cooed over him as much as she did the baby. And then he glanced around the room, realizing two people he expected to be up and greeting him hadn't yet. At first, he thought his best friend, and Penny weren't even there.

Then, he found them.

Tucked away in the corner of the room, Luca and Penny napped on chairs where they sat side by side. A blazer—Luca's, he knew—had been thrown over Penny's shoulder, and all that peeked out from her makeshift blanket was the color of her white-blonde hair.

"They went a bit crazy yesterday," his father explained, his attention half on Naz, and half on the baby that his grandfather, Dante, was holding. "Wanted to make sure you and Roz didn't have anything to worry about when you went home, so they cleaned, and took care of stuff outside, you know."

Huh.

That was mildly interesting.

And sweet.

He appreciated it.

What Naz found *more* interesting was the fact that Penny was using Luca's shoulder as a pillow. She had *turned away* from the rest of the room in her sleep, and more toward Luca. That was entirely unlike the young woman—not that she wouldn't let people touch her, she did—for a hug, or a handshake, but very little else—although he knew she was uncomfortable with it. It was more that she didn't let *men* touch her, and certainly not in a friendly way.

And yet, there she was.

Even in her sleep … he didn't think she would do that unless she wanted to.

When had that happened?

Naz tried to run over the last few months in his mind since Penny had come to stay with them. More than once, Penny and Luca had been in the same room, or around each other. Once or twice, he picked her up from school and dropped her off at the house if something came up. But nothing felt out of the ordinary there, and he couldn't draw back to a time when it felt or seemed like *more* than just Luca doing him a favor.

Penny was still seventeen.

Would be until the coming fall.

She hadn't decided *what* she wanted to do after high school quite yet, and they didn't push. Sometimes, people just needed extra time to work on themselves, and he and Roz had already settled on making sure Penny had exactly that for as long as she needed. The girl never had a safe place to land before them, so they didn't mind being it.

His friend, though …

Luca had a solid *six years* on her seventeen. He knew what Penny had been through in her young life. He didn't think his friend would cross a line with Penny … certainly not in *that* way, anyhow.

Maybe he was making more of two people sleeping on chairs than he should. Maybe nothing had happened at all. Maybe something *was just starting* to happen.

That felt … *right.*

Like he was seeing the beginnings of something, and perhaps he had been the first and only person to notice it.

Huh.

"Her graduation is in a week," Naz said.

"Hmm, son?"

"Penny. Her graduation is in a week."

Cross smiled. "I suspect it is going to be a busy next few days, then."

Yeah.

He thought so, too.

As for the Luca thing …

Well, Naz figured might as well wait it out and see what happened. If anything did, of course. Who could say one way or the other?

But *shit.*

Didn't that girl deserve to be happy?

He thought so.

It was the *hows* of it all that concerned him, but he figured ... well, the details weren't for him to work out. That was on them.

"What about Junior?" someone asked. "To differentiate?"

"No one is calling my namesake *Junior*," his father muttered.

"Fine, Cross, *Jesus*."

Naz's attention went back to his family. He could deal with whatever else another time. This was more important.

And Roz.

Her, too.

"You feeling good?" he asked his girl.

She beamed up at him, still tucked into his side. "Perfect, Naz."

Well, that was the goal.

TWENTY-TWO

Roz

The thing people warned about newborns, but couldn't truly be appreciated until one experienced it?

The exhaustion.

No lie, Roz was dead on her feet.

Two days of having her baby home, four days of little Cross being on this earth, and she wished more often than not that she had appreciated her ability to sleep for more than a spread of two hours at a time before he was born.

Oh, she *loved* her boy.

With every fiber of her being.

The truth was still the truth at the end of the day, and the truth was that she was tired. Breastfeeding every hour on the hour for the first two days hadn't seemed that bad when she was in the hospital with nurses, and a lactation consultant at her beck and call. There were people willing to take the baby out of the room for a bit of time, if she needed to shower or whatever else the case may be.

They had help.

At home?

Not so much.

Well, that wasn't entirely the truth. Her parents came over in the daytime to help, and so did Naz's mother and father. They had enough frozen casseroles to last them six months, at least, from people dropping off food as a *just in case*. She understood why now, because they were either too tired to cook for themselves, and would just order in, or they didn't have time between finishing one feeding just to start another.

Worth it, though.

God, it was all worth it.

And then Roz blinked up at the white ceiling of her bedroom, seeing the beginnings of sunlight dancing across the space, and realized ... the last time she opened her eyes, it was dark. Panic saturated her insides as she rolled over in the bed, wondering how long she had been asleep, and where in the *hell* was her son?

She breathed slightly easier when she found the clock on her nightstand blinked *six*. In the morning, that was. So, only two hours from the last feeding.

That was good, right?

It meant little Cross was spacing out his feedings more.

They said that might happen.

But where was he?

Because he wasn't in the bassinet next to her bed where he should be. Roz didn't even bother to worry about her full bladder, or the fact she should probably use that quiet time to roll over and get a little more sleep.

No, instead she crawled out of bed, found her robe hanging off the end, and wrapped it around her shoulders before padding out of the room. As soon as she came out into the hallway of their upstairs, she could hear familiar *tinkling*.

A tune she didn't recognize, but the notes rang loudly in her heart and mind. She appreciated the sound of the piano echoing through the house for a moment—likely Penny practicing, as she was considering an attempt at an audition for a ballet company in New York that wanted a pianist for a spread of shows they had coming up over the year. A risky move, but they wanted something different, if Roz understood it right.

Penny thought it might be cool—a break from finishing high school before she went into college, although she still hadn't picked what she wanted to do. And it allowed her to get back into music without ... well, the stress of something like Roz had chosen to do.

Roz fully expected to find Naz downstairs with the baby in the kitchen, or napping on the couch, and Penny at the piano. She was *partly* right, and a little bit wrong. She found Naz leaning in the entryway of the back sunroom which doubled as a music room, the baby grand piano resting proudly in the middle, sparkling.

Penny was, in fact, at the piano.

But so was their son.

Swaddled, tucked in her lap on the bench, with blinking eyes staring up at the girl as she played the piano for him, the baby seemed happy and content. Penny, either unknowing of her audience, or not caring, continued to play the piano.

Little Cross *loved* his bear with the song that Penny had recorded to put in the stuffy. In fact, it was the only way he would sleep in his bassinet. They *had* to turn it on, and sometimes let the music play through twice, and then he was happy to fall asleep.

She wasn't shocked he enjoyed listening to Penny play like this, too.

"Didn't want to wake me up?" she asked.

Naz gave her a smile as she came to stand with him in the doorway. "Well, you needed to sleep … and he does okay with those big nipple bottles you bought."

Yeah, lucky them.

The baby didn't get confused.

It meant Roz could express milk, if she wanted, and have Naz feed the baby using the bottles that were meant for breastfed infants. That way, she could get an extra hour of sleep here and there, but she still preferred to feed her son herself. The lactation consultant warned not to use the bottles too often, lest the baby find he preferred them, so Roz was willing to use them on occasion.

"Anyway, she was practicing," Naz said, "and he kept turning his head like he was trying to find the sound, so I brought him to her."

"Oh?"

"He helps her, too."

"How so?"

"She thinks less when she's holding him."

"How do you know?"

Naz shrugged. "I just do."

Roz didn't question him on it.

Naz was who he was.

Leaning against his side, he pulled her closer, and rested his chin on the top of her head while they watched the two across the room.

She was still tired, sure … but that was okay. This was the best way she had spent a morning in a while.

• • •

"Penny Dunsworth!"

Roz and Naz—and well, the whole row of people sitting beside them—were on their feet to clap for Penny as she crossed the stage in her green and gold graduation gown and cap to accept her diploma. Well, she tried to clap, but it was difficult when she had to hold the sleeping newborn in her arms at the same time.

That was okay.

Their family clapped loud enough for all of them.

This whole day …

That girl …

Eight months ago, this seemed impossible. Like Penny would never make it to this point, because a lot of the time, they weren't even sure if she was going to make it to the next *day*. That was her struggle—they never diminished it because it wasn't their battle to fight, and just because they didn't understand it didn't mean it wasn't real.

But *God*.

Roz was so proud of her.

"Forty-five," Naz murmured beside her.

Roz glanced up at him. "Forty-five what?"

"Arrests."

"What?"

Naz smiled, his gaze meeting hers as Penny took the diploma from her male principal *without* shaking the man's hand or accepting the hug he tried to offer. She turned a bit on the stage, waving a hand to their row who was only three back from the stage.

Roz smiled back.

"Forty-five arrests in two months since I made a program to crawl the dark web because of what happened to her," Naz explained, "and those are just the arrests that came from my program. Another ten came from names she gave me directly. It seems like a lot, but in the grand scheme, it's only a small portion. But in those forty-five arrests, over three-hundred children have been identified across the world from their activities, and are now safe, and getting help."

"Why didn't you tell me? That's amazing."

And *dangerous*, she was sure.

Not that it mattered.

"Because it's not about me. That wasn't ever about me."

"Does she know?"

Naz nodded. "Keeps track, actually."

Huh.

Roz glanced back at the stage just in time to see Penny walk off and rejoin the rest of her graduating class where she would stay until the end of the ceremony. "So, what happens now?"

"That's the best part."

"Is it?"

"Yeah, babe, because it's *anything*. Anything can happen now."

Well, then ...

Roz held her son tighter.

She couldn't wait.

ABOUT THE AUTHOR

Bethany-Kris is a Canadian author, lover of much, and mother to four sons, two cats, and three dogs. A small town in Eastern Canada where she was born and raised is where she has always called home. With her boys under her feet, a snuggling cat, barking dogs, and a spouse calling over his shoulder, she is nearly always writing something ... when she can find the time.

Find Bethany-Kris at her:

WEBSITE: www.bethanykris.com
BLOG: www.bethanykris.blogspot.ca
FACEBOOK: www.facebook.com/bethanykriswrites
TWITTER: @BethanyKris
INSTAGRAM: www.instagram.com/bethany.kris
PINTEREST: www.pinterest.com/bethanykris

Sign up to Bethany-Kris's New Release Newsletter here: http://eepurl.com/bf9lzD.

OTHER BOOKS

Renzo + Lucia

Privilege
Harbor
Contempt

Andino + Haven

Duty
Vow

John + Siena

Loyalty
Disgrace

Cross + Catherine

Always
Revere
Unruly
The Companion
Naz & Roz

Guzzi Duet

Unraveled, Book One
Entangled, Book Two

DeLuca Duet

Waste of Worth: Part One
Worth of Waste: Part Two

Standalone Titles

Effortless
Inflict
Cozen
Captivated
Dishonored

Donati Bloodlines

Thin Lies
Thin Lines
Thin Lives
Behind the Bloodlines
The Complete Trilogy

Filthy Marcellos

Antony
Lucian
Giovanni
Dante
Legacy
A Very Marcello Christmas
The Complete Collection

THE NAZ AND ROZ CHRONICLES

Seasons of Betrayal

Where the Sun Hides
Where the Snow Falls
Where the Wind Whispers
Seasons: The Complete Seasons of Betrayal Series

Gun Moll Trilogy

Gun Moll
Gangster Moll
Madame Moll
The Chicago War

Deathless & Divided
Reckless & Ruined
Scarless & Sacred
Breathless & Bloodstained
The Complete Series
Maldives & Mistletoe

The Russian Guns

The Arrangement
The Life
The Score
Demyan & Ana
Shattered
The Jersey Vignettes

Find more on Bethany-Kris's website at www.bethanykris.com

www.ingramcontent.com/pod-product-compliance
Lightning Source LLC
Chambersburg PA
CBHW061246170626
46809CB00007B/2865

* 9 7 8 1 9 8 8 1 9 7 8 9 0 *